Madalyn wondered what she'd gotten herself into.

She didn't want to admit how nervous Philip's proximity made her. She tried to tell herself it was because he was her new boss, not because he was so devastatingly handsome.

She reminded herself of what she'd accomplished by not letting emotion guide her decisions.

Actually, she'd let her emotions guide her once, but she'd learned....

Which was why she wasn't going to read anything into this business trip. Except when she remembered the blaze of passion she'd seen in his eyes when she thought he was going to kiss her last night...and her own traitorous response.

Well, it wasn't a problem, because she wouldn't be with him in any situation remotely intimate again. She'd make sure of it. Even if there was an irresponsible, rebellious piece of her wishing for just one little kiss to satisfy her curiosity....

Dear Reader,

Silhouette Romance blends classic themes and the challenges of romance in today's world into a reassuring, fulfilling novel. And this month's offerings undeniably deliver on that promise!

In *Baby, You're Mine*, part of BUNDLES OF JOY, RITA Award-winning author Lindsay Longford tells of a pregnant, penniless widow who finds sanctuary with a sought-after bachelor who'd never thought himself the marrying kind...until now. Duty and passion collide in Sally Carleen's *The Prince's Heir*, when the prince dispatched to claim his nephew falls for the heir's beautiful adoptive mother. When a single mom desperate to keep her daughter weds an ornery rancher intent on saving his spread, she discovers that *McKenna's Bartered Bride* is what she wants to be...forever. Don't miss this next delightful installment of Sandra Steffen's BACHELOR GULCH series.

Donna Clayton delivers an emotional story about the bond of sisterhood...and how a career-driven woman learns a valuable lesson about love from the man who's *Her Dream Come True*. Carla Cassidy's MUSTANG, MONTANA, Intimate Moments series crosses into Romance with a classic boss/secretary story that starts with the proposition *Wife for a Week*, but ends...well, you'll have to read it to find out! And in Pamela Ingrahm's debut Romance novel, a millionaire CEO realizes that his temporary assistant—and her adorable toddler—have him yearning to leave his *Bachelor Boss* days behind.

Enjoy this month's titles—and keep coming back to Romance, a series guaranteed to touch *every* woman's heart.

Mary-Theresa Hussey

Mary-Theresa Hussey
Senior Editor

Please address questions and book requests to:
Silhouette Reader Service
U.S.: 3010 Walden Ave., P.O. Box 1325, Buffalo, NY 14269
Canadian: P.O. Box 609, Fort Erie, Ont. L2A 5X3

BACHELOR BOSS

Pamela Ingrahm

Silhouette
R O M A N C E™
Published by Silhouette Books
America's Publisher of Contemporary Romance

To my agent, Linda Kruger.
What a joy it has been working with you!
Here's to many more years
and many more books.

 SILHOUETTE BOOKS

ISBN 0-373-19401-3

BACHELOR BOSS

Copyright © 1999 by Paula D'Etcheverry

Visit us at www.romance.net

Printed in U.S.A.

Books by Pamela Ingrahm

Silhouette Romance

Bachelor Boss #1401

Silhouette Desire

Cowboy Homecoming #964
The Bride Wore Tie-Dye #1038
Wedding Planner Tames Rancher! #1086
The Texas Ranger and the Tempting Twin #1170

PAMELA INGRAHM

lives in Austin, Texas, with the man of her dreams and their two children. She's added to the mix one dog that thinks the human race was put here to love her, and Pamela swears she's not doing anything to foster that notion. She also tells all who will listen how wonderful it is to live your dream.

Chapter One

As far as birthdays went, Madalyn Wier had had better.

If there was one thing that would salvage being thirty, a single mother and facing unemployment, it would be landing an executive assistant position at Ambercroft, Inc.

Madalyn craned her head back to look at the massive building standing as a testament to old money and exemplary architecture. The tip of the hundred-story-plus structure pressed into the Dallas sky, as if to say heaven itself made room for the Ambercrofts.

Crossing her arms against the brisk spring wind, she waited for traffic to clear. Obviously, the hospitality Texans were known for disappeared after four o'clock during the work week. At least in downtown Dallas....

Once across the street, she paused outside the

heavy, leaded glass doors and adjusted her suit jacket. With a deep breath, she went inside and moved confidently to the reception desk…or as close to confident as she could manage. At least she hoped she looked confident.

The first thing that struck her as she waited for the receptionist to acknowledge her was that the woman looked agitated. While Madalyn knew well how harrying the job could be, somehow showing it didn't seem…Ambercroft-ish.

She gave the woman time to answer a crush of phone calls and glanced around the lobby. Marble floors polished to a diamond sheen ended in walls of dark wood. A section of marble stretching to the vaulted ceiling framed the portraits of five generations of Ambercrofts, each representative impeccably dressed in a dark suit. The styles themselves were a statement to the duration of the family legacy, and it was a bit unnerving to be stared at by the daunting figures. Madalyn assumed that was the point—to make sure all visitors knew they were entering a bastion of power.

With each successive generation, the men became more handsome, but somehow increasingly stern. Until the portrait of the youngest, Philip Ambercroft. Philip Ambercroft IV, to be exact. While being by far the most handsome, he alone wore a Mona Lisa smile that easily caught her attention. Maybe it was because she'd seen so many photographs of him in everything from news weeklies to the tabloids, or maybe it was just her imagination, but he seemed to want the viewer to wonder just what was going on behind that intelligent face.

At a break in the incessant but muted ringing, Madalyn stepped forward. "Excuse me—"

"Ms. Fox is away for a minute. I'm from Accounting and just—" The woman jabbed at the telephone and gave Madalyn a less than warm look, as if the new call was her fault. "Reception. No, please hold." Jab. "What do you need?"

"I'm here to apply for a position with—"

Jab. "Reception. Please hold."

"—Mr. Ambercroft?"

"Mr. Ambercroft is on the twenty-first floor."

"I'm afraid you've misunderstood—"

The ersatz receptionist held the receiver away from her ear and pinned Madalyn with a glare. "I said twenty-first floor."

Recoiling from the angry, haughty look, and in no mood to argue, Madalyn headed for the bank of elevators nestled in granite. Maybe someone on the twenty-first floor could direct her to the personnel office with a bit more tact and grace.

It was at times like these that Madalyn wished she could take the risk and open her own nursery. At least roses and ficuses didn't glare at you and get snippy. But that old dream was out of reach. She needed a steady paycheck and benefits now that she had more than just herself to think of.

The elevator ride up was smooth and quick, but then again, she was in the Ambercroft building, and machinery didn't dare perform less than perfectly. When the doors slid open, she stepped out onto a sea of mint-green carpet that felt as though it had a mile of padding underneath. She allowed herself an entire minute of slack-jawed awe. A vacant secretary's desk sat in front of her, bigger than any executive's desk she'd ever seen, and state-of-the-art everything was neatly arranged on the exquisitely grained wood. The guest couch and chairs whispered upholstered elegance and the door off to the left fairly bellowed that this was the entrance to the inner sanctum.

Madalyn stifled a giggle when she envisioned a sleekly polished Miss Moneypenny type sitting behind that desk. But no Miss Moneypenny sat there now, and Madalyn was fairly certain this wasn't the personnel department.

She was about to turn around and head back to the first floor to try again, when the door to the inner sanctum opened. Somehow, the way this day had gone, it didn't surprise her in the least that Philip Ambercroft came out with a harried expression on his face, engrossed in something on the page he was holding.

He was so much more striking in person than in print, or oil and canvas for that matter, that Madalyn was startled. She'd heard the expression *chiseled* to define someone's features before, but he was the first person she'd met who truly fit the description. European royalty was all she could think of to conceptualize the thoughts whirring through her head, but from what she knew through her extensive reading, she doubted such fiercely proud Americans as the Ambercrofts would appreciate the analogy. In fact, they were just as fiercely Texan.

He was almost on top of her before he pulled up short. He gave her a quick glance and turned toward the desk, his jaw snapping shut when he didn't find the person he so obviously expected to be there.

"Just have a seat. I'll be right back."

Without another word, he entered the elevator and punched a button, leaving Madalyn with the lingering trace of his crisp, clean cologne.

When she finally remembered to breathe, she took a seat as instructed. She didn't have much choice. Her knees had just given out.

Not five inches from her. Philip Ambercroft had been not five inches from her. She'd been close enough to see the light-colored flecks in his blue eyes. She could have reached out and touched the lock of midnight-black hair that had fallen rakishly over his forehead and discovered if it was as velvety soft as it looked. Her fingertip could have traced the slight bow of his strong, upper lip—

"Get a grip, Madalyn!" She said the words aloud to give them more impact. The fact that her fingers trembled as she swiped them across her forehead didn't give her much confidence. She had to get herself together before she blew it completely.

Praying Mr. Ambercroft would stay gone for a few minutes, she worked on composing herself. The open position was with Gene Ambercroft, not Philip, so that was two mistakes she could thank the pseudo-receptionist for—the wrong floor and the wrong Ambercroft, but there was no sense in getting frustrated. She could just chalk it up to a day full of frustrations.

Now that she'd seen him, in the flesh, she couldn't

get her mind off Philip Ambercroft. She could admit in the privacy of her own mind that she—along with about ten million other Americans—had an intense curiosity about the Ambercrofts. They were American royalty, and the press treated them accordingly.

Unlike the female population of America, though, she was fascinated by the business tycoon Philip, not his playboy brother. She wouldn't mind working for Gene, but it was the oldest Ambercroft brother who had captured her imagination from the first article she'd ever read on the famous family.

There was something about him, something intriguing, that was so much more interesting than mere sex appeal. While definitely as sexy as his baby brother, Philip was the one who exuded confidence and grace, not mere raw testosterone—at least in her opinion. She decided that wasn't really fair to Gene. It was the reporters who concentrated on his dating life. She doubted anyone really wanted their every move cataloged in a magazine, although Gene knew how to play the paparazzi and keep them among his adoring throng. They didn't seem to bother him here at home, but loved to follow him abroad.

Reporters did their fair share of cataloging Philip's dates, but Philip didn't have the patience Gene seemed to have. He considered it an infringement on his privacy and often said so. While Madalyn admitted that she envied the tall beauties pictured on his arm, she had the feeling an evening with Philip would be as absorbing intellectually as it was stimulating, and would be worth a hassle with the press.

Reminding herself she needed to get out of there

before Philip returned, she picked up her purse and folder and prepared to find the personnel office. This was a chance of a lifetime, and she didn't intend to blow it. If she had the choice, she'd work for Price Manufacturing forever, but that wasn't possible so the issue was moot. Mr. and Mrs. Price were like surrogate parents to her, and surrogate grandparents to Erin, and her concern for them was just one more reason she wanted this job. She didn't want the Prices worrying about her when they had enough troubles these days. The Prices had a whole company of loyal employees they were about to have to let go, while she only had Erin to worry about.

Just thinking about Erin made Madalyn smile. She still wasn't sure how just three years ago she'd been positive she never wanted children. Now, of course, she couldn't imagine life without her precious daughter.

But now was not the time to be reflecting on the not-quite-two-year-old pixie who took up her every spare moment. Now was the time to be concentrating on getting a job that would provide the little pixie with a home and day care and clothes and food....

Just as Madalyn reached for the elevator button, the bell chimed and the doors opened. She stepped back with renewed aplomb.

"Mr. Ambercroft," she said, acknowledging him as she prepared to slip by. "Excuse me."

His brow furrowed in confusion. "Where are you going?"

"Going?"

"Yes. Isn't that file for me?" he asked, nodding toward her arm.

She knew from her contact at the employment agency that Philip would be making the final decision on the applicants, which seemed a bit odd to her, but maybe it was because Gene was out of the country. In the end, it wasn't something to worry about. Yet she hadn't expected Philip to be quite so involved at this stage.

"Well, I...suppose it is, in a way...."

He reached for the file, his fingers brushing her arm as he took it from her grasp. The sensation flustered her, making her forget what she was going to say.

She watched, speechless, as he opened the folder and read for a moment. Another frown crossed his forehead.

"What's this?" he asked, glancing up. "Where's the Ashton Hills report?"

"Ashton Hills?"

"Aren't you from Denham's office?"

"Um...no, I'm—"

"If you're not from Denham's office, what are you doing here?"

"I'm here about the executive assistant position open for Mr. Ambercroft."

His whole demeanor changed instantly. His back straightened, the hint of a smile that had been playing at the edge of his mouth disappeared and he gave her a once-over that bordered on offensive. He seemed to catalog every inch of her bust, the narrowness of her waist and the exact flare of her hips—as if he could see through the boxy cut of her fashionable but reserved suit. His eyes made a slow sweep of her legs before coming back to her face.

"I'm sorry, Miss—" he glanced at her résumé again "—Price."

"I currently work for Price Manufacturing. My name is Madalyn Wier."

The man stopped short again, but Madalyn couldn't begin to guess what he was thinking. She had the distinct impression he'd just done another mercurial shift, but she was clueless as to why a bit of the warmth returned to his face. Now he was reading her résumé as if he hadn't seen it before.

This time, when he looked up, the smile was back, but she would have bet her last nickel that something significant had changed. It wasn't in the curve of his lips; it was in his eyes, eyes that said he missed little.

"Ms. Wier, I apologize for the mix-up. Would you come into my office? I'd like to get this straightened out."

He didn't give her a chance to waver. He came closer and took her elbow, ushering her politely toward his door.

Madalyn's breath caught again at his touch, and she had to concentrate on putting one foot in front of the other without tripping. She could only hope she appeared calm and professional on the outside, because her insides were a wreck. She had no choice, really, but to go along with Philip, and she offered a quick prayer that this impromptu interview would be just the break she needed.

Philip's mind was already whirling as he walked around his desk and took a seat while he studied her file with more care. When he was finished, he stalled for a bit more time by shuffling a pile of papers. He hadn't gotten where he was by being slow on his feet, and if he played this right, he might just salvage a week from hell and get some information on a company he had his eye on, to boot.

Philip didn't question the marvelous opportunities that had come to him over the years, events he could never have planned or predicted. He was, however, smart enough to act on them…immediately.

He'd been about to dismiss Ms. Wier out of hand—after all, she was much too attractive to even consider interviewing for Gene's position—when a plan started coming together. There were those who didn't think he had a heart, much less a libido, but Ms. Wier had already proven she could raise both his pulse and his…imagination. Feeling that instantaneous reaction, that unexpected response, hadn't happened in so very long, he couldn't help but be amazed. And it had certainly never happened with an employee.

But Ms. Wier's attributes weren't the point. The fact that she met so many needs at one time made her beauty serendipitous.

Number one, his secretary was on an extended leave, and he hadn't kept a temp for more than a day for the last week. One had walked out at lunch and never returned. One had been pregnant and gone into premature labor. One had taken ill with the stomach flu. He wasn't sure why his luck was running so sour in this area, but it was becoming a bit annoying.

Number two, Ms. Wier had an impressive résumé,

including a tenure with a company he had his sights on. Price Manufacturing would make a nice addition to the Ambercroft portfolio of companies.

Number three, he wanted more information before he made a move on Price Manufacturing, and who knew more about a company than an executive assistant?

Hell would freeze over, however, before he let his little brother hire a secretary like Ms. Wier. Gene had used Ambercroft, Inc., as his personal procuring service for the last time. When he came back from Europe with his latest secretary-turned-lover, he was going to find an efficient, talented and decidedly matronly secretary waiting for him. Philip had already thought of a few words to describe Ms. Wier, but matronly wasn't even in the same dictionary.

So, his most urgent needs were met in the attractive little package sitting patiently across from him with her hands folded in her lap. He'd have to do all the sensitive letters himself since his secretary wouldn't be back for at least a month, but he could get a mountain of correspondence on other matters dictated and off his desk. Surely, in the weeks remaining until Mrs. Montague returned, he could get caught up and possibly discover some interesting information about Price Manufacturing. Then, with Gene's secretary firmly replaced by a Mrs. Montague clone, he'd find a slot for Ms. Wier in one of Ambercroft's many departments, and his life would return to normal.

What more could he ask for?

A glance at the stockinged calf revealed beneath Ms. Wier's proper navy skirt gave a hint at exactly what more he could ask for—in the privacy of his own mind, of course. He'd never fraternized with an employee in his life, and he wasn't about to start now. That was Gene's department....

Yet, Philip doubted it would be a hardship to dictate to Ms. Wier's delicate, oval face. Mrs. Montague was a handsome woman, no doubt, but she was almost as old as his mother and not exactly his type. He respected Mrs. Montague a great deal, and valued her as an employee, but the sight of her ankle had never even come close to making his pants seem tighter.

Reining in his wandering thoughts, Philip pulled out another smile. "Your résumé says you take shorthand."

"Yes, I do," she affirmed, straightening slightly in her chair.

"Good, good. It's hard to find a secretary who knows shorthand these days. I confess I'm a holdout who hates those little tapes and prefers to dictate the old-fashioned way."

Her answer was a polite smile.

He folded his hands on his desktop and put on his "Let's get comfortable, shall we?" expression. "There seems to be a little misunderstanding here, but I think we can work this out. You see, my brother is in Europe right now and won't be back to interview for his position for several weeks, I'm sure."

He paused as a thought suddenly occurred to him. Why had the headhunters sent someone who looked like this to interview in the first place? He'd spoken personally with the head of the agency, making it clear exactly what he wanted in prospective candidates for the position. He'd offered a salary that was sure to bring in applicants with impeccable references and long years of experience. That usually meant someone older than thirty, and Philip had more like forty-five or fifty in mind.

So what was a woman like Ms. Wier doing here? The agency valued his business too much to ever make a mistake like that.

"Ms. Wier, how did you hear about our opening?"

Philip had watched too many people across a negotiating table to miss the tiny flicker in her eyes. Possible coup or not, if she lied to him—and he'd know—she was out on her cute little rear.

"To be honest, I heard through a friend-of-a-friend kind of thing. This is a job I'm highly qualified for, and I made the decision to take advantage of the valuable information."

He liked a person with initiative—to a certain point. He admired gumption in a competitor and in an employee, as long as they didn't push too far. He appreciated that she'd taken an opportunity, especially in this instance where it worked to his advantage, but he also made a note to watch her and make sure her proactive approach didn't end up biting him on the behind.

Although she had an excellent poker face, he could feel her tension. He waited just long enough to make his unspoken point before nodding.

"As a businessman, I can respect that." He reread her file and let his ambiguous response hang. "So tell me why you're leaving Price Manufacturing."

Before the words even came out of her mouth, he knew she was about to give him the prepared story. He hadn't turned over his family's measly ten million this many times without honing a certain amount of psychic skill.

"Mrs. Price wants to come back to work. She says she's bored, and after all, she ran the company with Mr. Price for years. They're a good team. Anyway, they told me to take as much time as I needed to find a good job, but once I was settled, Mrs. Price would take the office back over. They pride themselves on being a family-run operation, you know."

Yes, he knew. He knew Eva and Martin Price socially, and he knew their excellent reputation.

"Then I'm sure they will give you a good reference."

He let her sit a moment longer, waiting until she uncrossed her legs and recrossed them before continuing. "As I said, my brother won't be back for quite some time, but as it happens, my own secretary is out, and I need a temporary to stand in for her. Could I interest you in working for me for a few weeks? We'll call it a dry run, if you will. When Mrs. Montague returns, you may still wish to apply for the opening, but if that doesn't work out, I feel sure we can find a place for someone of your talent at Ambercroft, Inc."

Philip named a salary even higher than he'd offered the headhunters, making the money alone worth her while to take the temporary position. Sweetening the deal with a promise of permanent employment was mere icing. This way, everybody won. Even Gene, although Philip had no intention of his brother ever knowing about this little venture.

His watch gave a small beep and he glanced at his wrist. Only five o'clock? Good, he could still get some work done.

Ms. Wier shifted in her seat, recapturing his attention. He'd never hired an employee based on their physical appearance, but in her case, he just might be tempted to make an exception. He had always been fond of brunettes, and her green eyes were bright and inviting. She had the presence and grace that said she was completely unaware of the power of her classic features. She had a timeless beauty that reminded him of some of the stunning women who'd starred in the old movies he favored. Elizabeth Taylor in her prime, Katherine Hepburn, Ingrid Bergman.

To be practical, however, by hiring Madalyn he'd have much more than someone pleasing to look at. He'd have a qualified, motivated assistant.

"Well, Ms. Wier? What do you think?"

"I'm very interested, of course. I'd need to know if medical benefits are available during this...dry run...as you call it, and if vacation will begin to accrue."

He hid a smile. No overeager cream puff here. He was beginning to like her more and more. He despised ingratiating fools and pushovers.

"Medical, yes, we'll get you on the corporate policy right away. Vacation and sick time will begin once you're a permanent employee."

She nodded, as if expecting his response. "Then I'll say yes, Mr. Ambercroft."

Philip wasn't smug, but Gene wasn't the only Ambercroft who could be charming. "Please, if we're going to work together you must call me Philip. If I can call you Madalyn...?"

"Of—of course."

"Great." He shifted the folders on his desk and tossed a notepad and pen across to her. "Let's get started."

Chapter Two

Madalyn shook a cramp out of her wrist. Now she knew why they called Philip Ambercroft a tyrant!

Thank God her mother was visiting from Louisiana. She was lucky enough to have a private sitter who never worried about an exact pick-up time, and she had a cousin in town who was always delighted to get Erin in an emergency, but she hated to ask unless it was absolutely necessary. At least her guilt was somewhat mitigated by knowing Erin was with her grandmother—someone who worshiped the ground Erin toddled on.

She reminded herself not to complain. Even if it was a bit surprising to be put to work the same day as an interview—and at five o'clock in the evening at that—at least Philip was interested in her. And if she made a good impression, her future employment might just be sealed. He was by no means bound by what he'd said earlier, so she wanted to be darn sure to earn that permanent position.

She knew some called him ruthless, castigating him as a takeover tycoon, but she had read enough about him to know that while he wasn't totally altruistic, he did rebuild the floundering companies he bought and turned them into cash cows. She admired Philip's no-nonsense approach to business and his refusal to accept less than the best from his employees. She had scraped and pulled herself inch by inch out of the suffocating poverty of her hometown, and had gotten where she was by giving one hundred and ten percent at every job she'd ever had. Philip seemed like a boss who could appreciate that kind of work ethic.

As long as he didn't take advantage too often. She admitted she was a bit sensitive in this area, but she was working on not letting a past mistake color her whole future. Not every handsome boss was a lying snake in the grass.

Of course, now that she'd taken dictation steadily for over an hour, which still had to be typed up, a part of Madalyn wanted to tell him to take his job and…well, do something anatomically impossible with it. The thought was fleeting, and she nearly gave her desk a superstitious rap. She didn't want to jinx anything, even with an errant thought.

She didn't mind giving one hundred and ten percent, but today was her birthday. Her mother was waiting to go out for Chinese food, and then they were going to take turns arguing over who got to hold Erin while they watched the movie Madalyn had rented the night before. It probably wasn't most people's idea of a big birthday bash, but it suited her just fine.

Madalyn glanced at the clock. It was almost seven and she wasn't even close to being finished. Picking up the telephone, she sighed and dialed her home number. She brushed a wayward strand of not-quite brown, not-quite-red hair out of the way as she pressed the receiver to her ear.

Her mother's Cajun accent jarred her out of her wandering thoughts.

"Et?"

"Hi, Mom, it's me again. Looks like we have to cancel my birthday plans. I'm not even close to getting out of here."

"You're still working? My goodness!"

"I'll tell you all about it when I get there, but that may not be for a while. Don't let me forget to call Mr. Price at home and let him know what happened."

"I'll write you a note. I'm sorry about tonight, shay. But my angel and I are having a good time."

"Oh, yeah? And how many cookies has she conned you out of?"

"Don' you talk about my angel that way!"

"Mother…"

"Just three, but they were just a bit and a piece—"

"Mother, don't you dare give her another one. Has she eaten any dinner at all?"

"Yes, and had a bath, and she's rubbin' her little eyes. I swear she looks like your papa lookin' back at me."

Madalyn smiled. "I know, Mama. Listen, I've got to go. I'll see you soon. Kiss my sweetie for me."

"Sho' thing. You drive home careful, he'ya?"

"Yes, I hear. Love you."

Madalyn hung up, her good humor restored. With her usual determination, she faced the computer screen and typed the pages of dictation she'd taken. Once she was in the groove, she lost track of time again, and it was only when she realized she was in danger of a permanent crick in her neck that she stopped and stretched.

"Madalyn?"

Philip's voice startled her, making her heart race. She hadn't even heard him open his door.

"I'm sorry I've taken such advantage of you on your birthday. I was looking over your résumé again and the date finally struck me."

She tried to make her smile sincere. "That happens sometimes. It's not the end of the world."

"Still, I've thrust you straight into the lion's den and didn't even think about the time. Let me take you to dinner to make up for it."

"Oh, no, that's not necessary—"

"I insist. What do you like? Chinese? Mexican?"

"I love Chinese, but—"

Madalyn paused, sensing a challenge in his voice. Good heavens, hadn't she proven already that she was a team player? A cold fear settled in her stomach, and she hoped she hadn't misjudged Philip—she hoped he wasn't the philandering type. But then, she'd misjudged before…

"Philip, listen, I have to be up-front with you." She took a deep breath, hoping she wasn't about to put herself out of a job. "I'm not comfortable mixing business with social events. I appreciate the offer and all, but I'd rather not.''

He looked surprised, but nodded graciously.

"Very well, then. Why don't you get out of here and salvage what's left of your evening?''

"I appreciate that. I'm close to being done, so I'd like to finish these letters so we can start fresh tomorrow. If that's all right.''

"That's not necessary—''

"Really, I'd rather. It shouldn't take me but an hour or so. I'm on a roll. Unless I'm keeping you?''

"Not at all. I appreciate the offer.''

He retreated again into his office, and his phone line lit up almost immediately. It only served to heighten her image of Philip at his desk seven days a week. She didn't need her insider info to know that he was a driven man; that was the first thing any article said about him. Now that she'd met him in person, his drive emanated from him in a palpable wave. She wondered for a moment just what she'd gotten herself into, and decided just as quickly that she'd work weekends without complaint, if he asked, for the experience this was going to provide her, and the security it would give her and Erin.

She wasn't sure what could have surprised her more, a mere forty-five minutes later, when the elevator door opened and a man came in bearing white plastic bags. The smells emanating from the bags made her stomach grumble, and she didn't have to be able to read the red symbols on the outside of the bags to know a feast had just been delivered from

Woo Duck Fong's Chinese Emporium. Fong's was her favorite restaurant in the whole world.

Philip must have heard the commotion, for his door opened and he took care of the delivery guy with a minimum of fuss. She watched, amusement warring with concern.

"Philip—"

"Nope, no arguments. I've worked you like a slave driver on your birthday. I didn't mean to make you uncomfortable with my invitation, so I did the next best thing."

While he was speaking, he'd been pulling out little boxes and covered bowls. He moved files from her desk to the floor to make room.

"You really shouldn't have."

A smile transformed his face, making her heart turn over.

Maybe this wasn't such a good idea. Maybe she should keep looking until she found a kind, toad-faced man who was at least five inches shorter than her to work for. Anyone but a tall, dark man with a smile that could light up entire rooms at a time.

Madalyn didn't want to admit how nervous his proximity made her, and she tried to tell herself it was because he was her new boss, not because he was so devastatingly handsome. It was nearly eight o'clock at night and the man's suit looked as fresh and crisp as if he'd just put it on. She, on the other hand, felt rumpled and wrinkled, which was not unexpected after the day she'd had. Her suit jacket was hanging on the back of her chair and now she wished she hadn't taken it off.

Giving herself a stern mental rap on the knuckles, she told herself to be gracious, eat the food that was making her mouth water and then get home.

"Thank you for the dinner. It smells great. But how did you know Fong's is my favorite?"

"Isn't it everybody's?" he asked, his expression teasing. "The truth is, I had no idea, but you said you loved Chinese, and this is the best food this side of Hong Kong, so it made sense to me...."

Somehow she knew he wasn't speaking metaphorically. He'd probably been to Hong Kong a dozen times and knew exactly who served the best Chinese food this side of the Pacific.

Philip pulled one of the guest chairs closer to the desk and settled back with a carton of beef and broccoli.

"So tell me about yourself, your family." He grimaced and waved his chopsticks in the air. "Wait! Forget I asked that. My attorney said he'd have my head if I asked any personal questions of my employees."

She had to smile at his obvious disgust. "I take it you've been thoroughly warned about avoiding discrimination lawsuits."

Stabbing a bright green broccoli flower, he chomped it with a satisfied sigh before nodding. "Sometimes I think we've just about gone over the edge with political correctness. I hate having to guard every word I say."

Madalyn tilted her head to the side. "I'm surprised. With your business reputation, I'd think you'd be well-tuned to this stuff."

"This stuff, as you put it, is taking all the fun out of business."

"Well, don't worry. You didn't offend me, and I promise not to sue."

He returned her smile and leaned forward, reaching for a packet of soy sauce. "Good. So tell me about yourself, Madalyn Wier."

"What would you like to know?"

"Everything. Start with the usual, like where you're from, and we'll go from there."

Other than perfunctory information, she hardly expected true interest from him. After a few unimportant details, undoubtedly he'd carry the conversation. Which was fine with her, since he'd been a source of fascination for her for a long time. She wanted to know everything about him, and to have the ball in her court was slightly disconcerting.

"I was raised in a little town called Asulta, Louisiana."

"I've never heard of it."

She laughed. "Of course you haven't! It's a tiny little town, meriting a mere pinprick on a Rand-McNally map. We're far off the beaten path and miles from the nearest highway, so the only industry in our town is a couple of garment factories. Everyone worked for one or the other, except for the few folks like my father who worked for the school system."

"What did he do?"

"He was a janitor until he died when I was eight."

"I'm sorry."

"Sorry that he was a janitor or sorry he died?"

His lips curved in an answer to her cheeky question. When he smiled, his face was transformed from godlike perfection to a boyish charm that captivated her. It took yet another stern mental warning to remind her that she didn't need to be captivated by her new boss—even if he was just a temporary boss.

"I'm sorry that you lost your father," he clarified with definite sincerity in his voice, despite his teasing smile. "I lost my father when I was in college, and that was hard enough. I can't imagine being as young as eight."

"It was rough," she admitted without rancor. "I was a late-life surprise for my parents, so I have to confess I was fairly doted on."

His expression turned slightly ironic. "I can see we had vastly different childhoods."

"I'll say," she said with a laugh. "I'd never even seen a tennis court, except on television, until I was a teenager."

"That's not what I meant," he replied. "I'm just trying to picture my father as doting, and the image just won't gel."

"I'm not sure what I'm supposed to say," she admitted hesitantly. He'd startled her as she never expected something so personal to enter the conversation. Weren't negative family comments a no-no in the rich person's rule book?

Philip shook his head as if suddenly realizing what he'd said.

"Sorry about that," he said with a sheepishness that reached out and caught her imagination. "Didn't mean to get maudlin on you."

Maudlin wasn't the word she would have chosen.

Introspective, maybe, but that's what nabbed her attention so fully. The image she was getting of him conflicted with the picture she'd already drawn in her mind. She expected someone cold and calculating, someone who never looked at the past, yet she was facing someone quite charming with an undercurrent of power and magnetism that she would do well to not underestimate.

He put his entrée on the desk before shifting to casually rest his arm on the back of his chair. The move stretched his dress shirt across his chest, his jacket now discarded, and her mouth went a little dry. Good heavens, the man was dreamy! Maybe it was her imagination, but he bore an uncanny resemblance to her favorite actor, although Mr. Brosnan might argue the presumption. Still, with the five-o'clock shadow shading his face and his dark hair just ever-so-slightly mussed, she'd have to say that yes, indeed, Philip Ambercroft looked rather Bond-ish at the moment.

"So tell me about your favorite birthday memory," he said, startling her out of her wayward thoughts.

Wrinkling her brow, Madalyn tried to think. Favorite birthday?

"I guess it would be my eighth, just before my father died. A carnival was in a town close to ours and where my dad got the money, I have no idea, but we all went and rode every ride, ate every kind of junk food, and I got to ride the little Shetland ponies—you know, where they walk around slowly in a circle? Real excitement for a girl who'd never even seen a horse up close and personal. What about you?"

"Easy. I was sixteen and at boarding school in Switzerland. My parents couldn't make it over and I spent the entire weekend by myself on the slopes. No pressure, no one watching, no yardsticks."

"Your sixteenth birthday by yourself? That sounds sad."

"Not at all. It was the first time I felt like my birthday wasn't some kind of litmus test about my reaching my manhood."

He said *manhood* with such derision, she couldn't begin to imagine growing up under such pressure. The image was heart-wrenching, one he'd managed to convey in a sentence, and she was once again stunned by this very personal glimpse into a very private man's life.

"I'm sorry to hear that. Holidays are special to me. Especially Christmas and birthdays. Sounds like you could take 'em or leave 'em."

"Oh, not so. And forgive me for being so talkative. I don't know what's gotten into me tonight."

"Must be my talent at scintillating dialogue," she said drolly.

"Must be," he agreed, his tongue in his cheek.

"You'll have to remember where to come when you're depressed from now on. Just call me Dr. Madalyn."

"Well, Doctor, I think your dinner is getting cold so we'll have to finish the session another day."

"Oh, darn," she said with mock regret, digging in to her orange chicken again and taking a bite. She sighed with sheer pleasure and wiped her mouth with her napkin.

As they finished the soup and egg rolls, the conversation became light and mundane. They talked
about the building, about some of Ambercroft's di-
verse holdings—nothing she didn't already know
from her research. But it was fun to listen to him talk,
to watch his face brighten with pride. He really did
love his company, and the many philanthropic en-
deavors they were involved in.

He even mentioned the gala Eva Price was chairing
for the Pediatric AIDS League.

"Are you going?" She couldn't stop enthusiasm
from coloring her voice. How wonderful for Eva, to
grab a contributor the likes of the Ambercroft family.

"I haven't committed yet. Are you attending?"

"Um, yes," she said, now hesitant and unsure why.
"I'm sort of on the committee. I've done several with
Eva, and it's wonderful to be a part of such good
work."

"Then I'll just have to find that invitation and
RSVP, won't I?"

Not sure how she was supposed to respond, she
concentrated on the last of her fried rice. The food
had been great, and she'd enjoyed talking to Philip,
but Madalyn was ready for the evening to be over. It
had been a long day, she was tired and she wanted to
snuggle her baby for a few minutes before dropping
into bed. She thought about telling Philip about Erin,
but she didn't want to start another long conversation.

Philip surprised her when he began clearing the
desk.

"I can do that," she said, preparing to help.

"No. You shut down the computer and get your

things. It's time for the birthday girl to open her fortune cookie and then go home.''

Dutifully cracking the treat, she opened the little
slip of paper and immediately laughed.

"Come on, don't keep me in suspense.''

"It says, 'A new job awaits you.'''

"You're joshing me.''

She handed over the fortune, and he laughed with
her. "Well, I'm wondering about mine, then. It says,
'You are next in line for a promotion.'''

She cocked her head. "Can the boss get a promotion?''

"Beats me. But I'll be sure to bring this to my next
board of directors meeting.''

With another round of laughter, they were ready to
call it a night. In no time, they were in the elevator
and headed for the parking garage. Philip had been
so polite the entire evening, it didn't surprise her
when he took the keys from her and opened her car
door. Still, she stood there, trying to display the
proper amount of righteous, feminist indignation. The
problem was, he'd moved so confidently, with such
arrogant smoothness, she forgot what she was supposed to do. All she could concentrate on was how
close he was, how alone they were, how soft his lips
looked. The awkwardness seemed to have vanished,
and for the merest second, it seemed he was bending
closer to her and she gasped. Yes, she wanted to kiss
him, wanted to see if he was everything her imagination promised—

Reality snapped back into place and they both
jerked away at the same time. Humiliation burned her

face and she fussed with her purse strap so she didn't have to look him in the eye. Maybe she could find a way to blame this on fatigue....

Wishing she could melt into the pavement, she managed to get in the car and strap her seat belt on.

"Good night, Madalyn," he said, shutting her door for her. "Sleep in tomorrow. You deserve it."

She wished she knew what he was thinking. Even more, she wished she could hide her feelings and thoughts as well as he could. She could only imagine the shade of red on her cheeks.

"Good night. And thank you again for dinner."

He nodded and stepped back so she could pull away, waiting until she'd disappeared from sight before going back to the elevator.

What the hell was wrong with him? When he'd called in dinner, he'd admitted it was a little unusual, but in his wildest dreams he'd never imagined that his secretary would turn him into a jabberjaw. He *never* talked about his childhood, and he never, ever talked about it with a stranger. But she'd tossed his questions back to him, and he'd responded, the words coming out of his mouth of their own volition.

Which was a huge sign that he needed to stay away from this woman in anything resembling a personal conversation. If she could turn what he had formerly considered his iron-clad control to mush this effortlessly, heaven forbid if she ever asked any really private questions. He'd probably rattle off his Swiss bank-account numbers.

Then his behavior by her car. He was sure he was certifiable after that move. But she'd been so close, and the faint trace of her perfume had made him forget who he was, who she was. All that he'd been thinking at that moment was that he wanted to kiss her, taste her, see if she was as perfect as she appeared.

Thankfully something had snapped him back. Now he had to make sure that this incident was never reprised.

He just hadn't expected to like her so much. He wasn't sure why, except maybe that while he had an extreme respect for Mrs. Montague, he'd never taken her or any other secretary out for a private dinner...although, technically, this dinner had been "in" not "out." Anniversaries and other special occasions were noted with bonuses and gift certificates for Mrs. Montague to enjoy with her family. It was a pattern that made them both comfortable.

But Madalyn had him thinking about sex—hot, hard, driving sex, and then slow, long and languorous sex—and all within hours of meeting her. It wasn't anything she'd done. Not one movement, not one look, not one word had been suggestive or inappropriate.

It was something primal that called to him past her proper demeanor. Then she'd unknowingly pricked his conscience when they'd spoken about the Price gala, and he'd felt himself withdrawing.

What had Sir Walter Scott said? "Oh, what a tangled web we weave..."

Suddenly he wasn't so sure working with her was such a good idea after all. Even if it meant not capturing Price Manufacturing, he decided having her so near was too risky. She messed with his equilibrium and he couldn't afford that; he wouldn't take that risk.

He had too much to do to be dealing with distractions by his own staff. Especially this kind of distraction. The best thing to do would be to cut his losses and get another temp. What was one more anyway, the way things had been going?

Feeling a pang of regret, he decided he'd have to break the news to her tomorrow.

Chapter Three

Madalyn was surprised to find Philip wasn't there when she arrived the next morning. A veteran early riser, especially now that she was a single mother, she hadn't taken him up on his offer to sleep in. She couldn't have, even if she'd wanted to. Erin's idea of sleeping in was letting the sun actually peek over the horizon.

She wasn't surprised, though, to see a stack of work neatly aligned on the corner of the desk. From the looks of it, he hadn't taken his own counsel to go home. He had to have been there past midnight to have gotten so much done.

She was grateful, though. On the drive in, she'd berated herself for being so determined to finish up last night. She feared having to sit there and twiddle her thumbs, which would have made her miserable. She supposed she should have known better. Philip was never idle, so why should his staff be? Besides, being busy made the day go faster, and it felt like she got home to Erin sooner.

By the time the elevator doors opened and he emerged, she was engrossed in a prospectus from Philip to the members of a joint venture interested in buying one of his companies. It should have been dry, dull work—inputting numbers into a spreadsheet, typing a long document from one of the tapes Philip had claimed to hate. Instead, she was intrigued.

"I thought I told you to sleep in."

Madalyn wished there had been a more teasing quality to his voice. "You did, but I'm not very good at that. It was hard enough waiting until nine to get here."

"Oh, well, yes, I appreciate your dedication. Listen, Madalyn…"

"Yes?"

"You see, about last night, I—"

The phone rang and she hesitated, picking it up when he gave an exasperated nod toward the phone.

"Mr. Ambercroft's office," she answered in a crisp, professional tone.

There was no response.

"Hello? May I help you?"

"Who is this?"

Madalyn told herself not to be put out by the imperious tone in the woman's voice. "I'm Madalyn Wier, Mr. Ambercroft's assistant."

"Of course," the woman said slowly. "Is my son in his office?"

"One moment please."

He raised an eyebrow as she put the call on hold.

"It's your mother," she said, answering his silent question.

Philip rubbed his forehead for a moment and when he dropped his hand, she thought she saw weariness in his incredibly blue eyes.

"I'll take it in here."

He disappeared into his office, shutting the door behind him. She understood his reaction. She loved her own mother dearly, and worried about her increasingly poor health, but no one on the face of the earth could exasperate her faster. She was grateful that her mother's visit had only produced one argument so far on Madalyn's single status. It was the only real source of contention between them. Their usual argument consisted of Madalyn trying to get her mother to move to Dallas so they could see each other more.

Philip came back out sometime later, and asked her about a file she had waiting for him. She stopped him when he turned to go back into his office.

"Was there something you wanted to say to me before we were interrupted?"

He looked at her for the longest time, the intensity of his gaze making her decidedly uncomfortable. It was almost as though he were battling himself, and she wondered if her own anxiety was what someone felt when facing a firing squad.

"No," was all he said before he shut his door behind him.

She didn't have to be hit on the head to understand that whatever subject he had been about to bring up was now closed and off-limits.

* * *

Philip leaned against his door, unaware until he looked down that he was crushing the file Madalyn had given him. After tossing the papers on his desk, he sat with controlled movements and leaned back.

First, he'd surprised himself by telling his mother more about Madalyn than that she was a temporary secretary. It had somehow slipped out that she had worked for Price Manufacturing, and even more startling, he'd said something about her amazing skills.

His mother's pause had spoken volumes. She was obviously as taken aback as he was to be discussing such mundane details with her. They weren't usually chatty.

Then he'd felt doubly foolish to hear his mother admonish him to not let his emotions interfere with his business sense. Since when had he needed his mother's advice? Not that she was ever hesitant to give it, but Philip had drawn the line years ago to remind his mother that not only was he nearly forty years old, but he was more than capable of making decisions without his mama's help.

He took responsibility for his actions, mistakes and all. Some lessons had been hard learned, such as losing his heart to Hannah Hollingsworth in college. That vivid lesson had made clear the fantasy of love conquering all. He hadn't thought it mattered that the Ambercrofts couldn't trace their roots to the *Mayflower*. They'd been proud, self-made Americans...even if they glossed over the fact that Grandfather Ambercroft was the one who had really boosted the family fortune by bootlegging whiskey during

Prohibition. As for himself, Philip thought his grandfather had been a hell of a guy, and he remembered listening intently to the stories the man had told about his youth. Philip suspected his grandfather had told the stories to irritate his mother as much as anything else.

But Hannah's family had a decided lack of humor, and put exorbitant pride in their mostly blue-blood ancestry, but he'd foolishly believed that wasn't enough to keep them apart. He'd begged her to run away with him, to marry him, and then they'd force her parents to accept him. But Hannah had been unable to defy her parents for a man they had considered well beneath them on the social register.

Philip was sure the day she'd refused him was the day his heart had frozen solid, as so many people believed to be true, and he'd vowed never again to let his emotions override his common sense.

Since then, he'd never let anything interfere with his goals. Now, all of a sudden, he's about to give up a lucrative business deal just because his new secretary—his temporary secretary—gave him a hard-on? Not bloody likely. He was going to get his brain and his libido under control and remember what he'd planned. He had no intention of doing anything illegal, or even immoral. When the time was right, he was going to flat-out ask her about Price Manufacturing. That was hardly diabolical.

He smoothed out the papers he'd wrinkled and sat down to put his mind to work with a ruthlessness that had made him the success he was. His eyes lost focus as his mind began to whirl. Price Manufacturing wasn't his pressing issue at the moment, so he set it aside. His present goal was McConnally Machinery.

He picked up the phone and punched out a number with quick, hard jabs.

When he'd finished his conversation, he felt a stiffness in his neck, but he ignored it as he hit the intercom. "Madalyn, would you come in here, please?"

"Yes, sir?" she asked a moment later from his doorway.

"Sit down."

She did as ordered and he was impressed at how well she hid her curiosity. Her demeanor was relaxed, her hands folded in apparent calmness, her expression open with a proper amount of question in her eyes.

He was going to go with his gut on this, for more than one reason, but he was depending on her experience as a high-level assistant in assuming she could maintain the poker face she'd displayed. If he was wrong, he might just kill two plans with one foul-up.

"Once again I'm springing something on you suddenly, but the negotiations on the file you just gave me have been moved up to tomorrow. On long sessions, such as this one will be, I usually take Mrs. Montague with me, as her note-taking skills are superb. Would you be willing, on this short notice, to fill in? I'd like to leave this afternoon, as things will start early in the morning. We'll be back late tomorrow."

She hesitated. Normally she couldn't have even considered his request as she wouldn't leave Erin with anyone overnight, but her mother was going to be there for at least another week.

"Is there a problem?" he prompted in the ensuing silence.

"I need to tell you something that I failed to mention yesterday. I have a child, and I'm a single parent."

"Oh," he said, not quite hiding a moment of surprise. "Of course, I understand then—"

"But it so happens that my mother is in town visiting, and if we'll only be gone one night, I don't see that it will be a problem. Where will we be going?"

Her matter-of-factness must have short-circuited his objections, for his tone became completely businesslike again.

"Mobile, Alabama. McConnally Machinery is the company. They machine ship propellers and shafts. I've been playing cat-and-mouse with the owner for a year now."

He opened the folder and handed her a black-and-white photograph of a man in his fifties, his silver hair combed back off his forehead. He had an open, engaging face, his skin slightly battered by years spent in the salty air and elements.

"His name is Connar McConnally. When you meet him, don't let his Southern, good-ol'-boy manners fool you. He likes to play the dumb hick, but this guy's sharp. His company is relatively small, but he's managed to keep a big chunk of the business on Mobile Bay all to himself. People whose very livelihoods depend on their boats being in the water will wait until this man—" Philip nodded toward the picture "—can get to their repairs. He started making noises about selling a year ago, but he won't play ball yet."

Madalyn studied the photograph and then handed it back across the desk. "What will I be doing for you there?"

"Be my eyes and ears. Do more than take notes. Watch people. Give me your impressions of their body language as well as their words."

"Do you think he's hiding something?"

Philip smiled. "Businessmen always have something to hide, but my interest lies in how big that something is. I think he's just smart enough not to appear too eager, but I want to make sure before we toss the first pitch. My goal is to talk him into letting Ambercroft take over, but get him to stay on and run things. I'm going to try and sell him on the idea that all he really wants is some of the burden taken off his shoulders, but this way he keeps the benefits of a company he's so proud of without the day-to-day worries."

"How do you plan to do that?"

"I know men like Connar. They don't really want to retire. Their work is their life and the thought of all that free time terrifies them. But they would like things to ease up—not too much, of course, or it wouldn't be fun anymore."

Madalyn nodded. "Sounds just like my dad. If he were alive, I'm sure he'd still be working, and he'd be in his seventies now." She gave her head a little shake, and her face returned to its former professional facade. "I'm sorry, I digressed. If we're leaving this afternoon, do I need to make any arrangements?"

"No. I have a travel office that takes care of these things. This is an easy trip as we own a hotel on the bay, as well as a casino in Louisiana and a condo complex in Florida. If we had time, we could do a little legal gambling.''

She smiled, as he'd hoped.

"Maybe next time," she said, but they both knew there wouldn't be a next time.

"The plane is getting prepped. Can you go home and get packed and be ready in two hours?"

"That will be plenty of time."

"Fine." He glanced at his watch. "I'll have my driver come pick you up at twelve-thirty so you don't have to leave your car in the garage. We'll meet at the airport."

He saw her hesitate as they stood, but was pleased when she nodded and walked out. He didn't want to notice how well her fashionably straight, above-the-knee skirt hugged her hips, how the short jacket made her waist seem impossibly small and how the silky stockings caressing her long legs made his fingers itch to touch.

He truly didn't.

But he had. In fact, his whole body had noticed— from the vein throbbing in his temple to the blood throbbing in...other...veins, making him shift away from the door in case she turned around.

He tried to get his mind back on business by replacing the photo in the folder and getting his briefcase packed.

It didn't work.

Madalyn hurried into her house in the little suburb she'd fallen in love with on the north side of Dallas, one of her carefully planned coups. The house had been owned by a company who had relocated an executive. They'd had it on the market for over a year with no takers. She'd offered an obscenely low bid, which in truth was just shy of all she could afford, and they'd come back with an absurd counteroffer. She'd countered back, and they'd taken it. She'd ended up in a house she normally could never have afforded, in a wonderful neighborhood, and was sure she had the lowest mortgage in a five-mile radius. Most of all, she was glad her little girl could grow up with grass under her feet and room to run.

With not a little disappointment that her mother and Erin weren't home, Madalyn pulled out her suitcase and started packing. The stroller was gone so she assumed they'd gone for a walk.

Her thoughts were whirring, especially about her agreement to go on this trip. She was proud of what she'd accomplished since leaving home, and she reminded herself that she'd done it all by keeping a cool head and not letting emotion guide her decisions.

Actually, she'd let her emotions guide her once, but she'd learned. Boy, had she learned....

Which was why she wasn't going to read anything into this sudden business trip. Philip hadn't mentioned travel in the interview, but that whole situation hadn't exactly been run-of-the-mill. The fact remained that her new boss was asking her to perform a business function, and she had no reason whatsoever to believe he had anything else in mind.

No reason except a blaze of passion she'd seen in

his eyes when she thought he was going to kiss her last night…and her own traitorous response.

Well, it wasn't going to be a problem because she wasn't going to be with him in any situation remotely intimate again. She'd make sure of it. Any hint of impropriety, and she'd set him straight in no uncertain terms.

Even if there was an irresponsible, rebellious piece of her wishing for just one little kiss to satisfy her curiosity, one little—

The front door slammed shut.

"Madalyn?"

"In here, Mom," she called back.

"I saw your car in the driveway. What are you doing home?" Carolina Wier asked, supporting a pink, snowsuited bundle on her hip.

The bundle's pixie face brightened, and her arms immediately came forward. "Mama! You home!"

Madalyn's heart swelled as she took her precocious daughter in her arms and twirled her around.

"Hiya, kiddo."

"Hiya diddo," Erin mimicked proudly.

"What have you two been doing?" Madalyn asked as she unzipped the one-piece snowsuit Erin had been wearing to protect her from the brisk spring winds.

"Meemaw walk."

Erin couldn't quite manage Grandma, so Meemaw had somehow become Carolina's designation.

Carolina captured a tailored blouse before it slid to the floor and gave Madalyn an arch look.

"I'm going on a business trip," Madalyn said to answer her earlier question. "That is, if you wouldn't mind handling Erin alone tonight. If you do, I'll cancel immediately. You know I wouldn't ask—''

"You know I don' mind one bit. But ain't this awful sudden?"

"Yes, it is. This whole situation has been a bit sudden. But I really want this job, Mom. And Philip is very polite and proper."

Except for that one moment by the car...but that didn't count, did it?

"Shay, you know I'm not monkeying in your business. You've done good by yourself these years. And if I can help, then I'm glad."

"Thanks, Mom. I'm truly sorry this is happening in the middle of our visit."

Carolina laughed. "Like I got anything waitin' for me at home but gators and skeeters."

Madalyn laughed. The mosquitoes so prevalent in her hometown were something of mythic proportion. "You have Aunt Elizabeth."

"Getting that old fool outta the house is like pulling coons' teeth. I ast her to come out he'ya with me."

Her mother's accent tended to get worse when she was agitated. Madalyn suppressed a smile. "Well, someday we'll get her to cross the Louisiana border. For now I've got to finish packing. The limousine will be here shortly."

"Limousine? Whoo yah, shay. Maybe you should pack that red fancy dress, too."

Madalyn gave her an indulgent look. "I'm his secretary, Mother, not his mistress. The red dress stays."

"I was just thinkin'..."

Madalyn's expression turned deeply serious. "Mom, I made a big mistake once thinking a boss could love a secretary. I'll never regret having Erin, but if I know anything at all, it's that fairy tales are just that. Tales. Bosses don't marry secretaries. Millionaires don't marry poor girls from tiny towns in Louisiana. So stop, okay?"

Carolina stepped closer and put a hand on her daughter's smooth cheek. "Forgive me, shay. I didn't mean—"

Madalyn patted her mom's knuckles and moved back to her packing. "I know you didn't, but you still believe all that stuff you told me as a little girl. How some day a prince is going to ride up and sweep me off my feet. That's just not going to happen."

Carolina picked up the now unrestrained Erin and gave her tummy a little tickle. "Don't give up hope, shay. That Keith Gutherie boy back home is still mighty in love with you. And his daddy just died and he owns half the parish."

Madalyn didn't try to change her mother's mind. It was beyond Carolina that a young, healthy—and in Carolina's eyes, absolutely beautiful—woman wouldn't have marriage as her highest priority. It was probably because despite never having more than two nickels to rub together, Carolina and Laymon Wier had been totally devoted to each other.

Madalyn wouldn't mind finding someone who would love her like that, who she could love just as much in return, but it didn't seem fate had the same plans for her.

Madalyn sat down on the bed and took the pins out

of her hair, shaking it loose from the French coil she consistently wore while working. The style was sleek and elegant, but more importantly, was easy to do. She brushed her hair absently, trying to get herself back on task. She had plenty of time left, but she didn't want to be rushing around when the limo arrived.

Besides, she wanted to squeeze every available second with Erin before she had to go. She knew it was only one night, but this would be the first time in Erin's twenty months on earth that Madalyn would be away for so long.

She couldn't get her mother's princess-waiting-for-a-white-knight image out of her head, though. "Oh, Mama," Madalyn said, looking into the mirror as she fixed her hair. "Why couldn't you have said, 'Madalyn girl, the best you can hope for is middle-class. Work your patootie off and save for a rainy day'?"

But no, she was stuck with the ridiculous dream that a man the likes of Philip Ambercroft would want to defy convention and run away with her.

Yeah, and pigs could fly.

By the time the driver beeped the horn to alert her to his presence in the driveway, Madalyn had restored herself to a modicum of sanity. She had even had a few free moments to read to her baby, then rock her to sleep for her nap.

She reminded herself fiercely, as she covered Erin's little legs with a soft blanket, that she had so much to be grateful for. She had a nice home, good skills and the most beautiful baby girl in the world.

There was no reason, no reason at all, for the hollow sadness around the area of her heart.

Chapter Four

Philip tried to concentrate on the numbers displayed on his laptop, and on the notes he was jotting on the pad on his knee, but somehow his attention kept shifting to Madalyn…who was making a valiant attempt to appear nonchalant as they winged their way eastward. There was something decidedly charming about her surreptitious examination of the cabin. He was used to the bored air affected by the few women he'd traveled with on the corporate jet.

Madalyn probably thought he jetted around the world on a whim. Not that he cared what Madalyn thought, of course, but for some reason he was fighting the urge to tell her that the jet was actually a fairly new purchase for the corporation. And ''jetting around'' to business meetings could actually get boring.

But he wasn't bored now. It was becoming damned

annoying that his pulse was up and his energy zooming—and all because of his secretary. His secretary, for heaven's sake! He must be coming down with a fever was all he could guess.

One part of him wished fervently Mrs. Montague would return from her vacation so his life would get back to normal. The other part, a very specific part, was much too enamored of the petite brunette fidgeting in the seat across from him.

"So, what do you think?" he asked suddenly, using his pen to indicate the airplane.

He felt guilty when she jumped as though he'd startled her.

"Oh," she said, a bit breathlessly, "it's...wonderful."

She laughed, and suddenly the tension eased in her shoulders. Her smile became genuine and a touch self-effacing.

"Philip, I'm going to make a confession that is hardly going to surprise you. I've never been in a private jet. Heavens, I've only flown commercially a few times in my entire life."

He pretended to be shocked, opening his eyes wide and raising his eyebrows, earning another grin from her.

She chuckled, hiding her lips behind her hand. "I keep expecting Ricardo Montalban to appear from behind that curtain back there to give us a lecture on rich Corinthian leather."

She stroked the butter-soft seat beside her thigh as she spoke, and his mouth went dry. The gesture was unconsciously sensual, her fingers tracing the topstitching, making him the one to shift uncomfortably. He set his pen and pad beside his computer before he knocked them to the floor with his suddenly less-than-steady hands. His head understood that it was her very lack of awareness of her sensuality that gave her so much power, but his libido wasn't nearly so logical.

He tried for humor. "I suppose Julia Child should squeeze through next to give us the in-flight menu?"

She giggled again. Strange, but giggling females usually annoyed him unbearably, but her smile, her willingness to be exactly who she was—void of affectation, natural—made her delightful.

"And then," she said, leaning forward as she joined the game, "we'll have a private concert by Kenny G."

He'd be damned if he didn't find himself laughing with her. Come to think of it, he'd laughed more in the last two days than he had in... Well, just how long? He couldn't remember the last time he'd wanted to simply talk with someone, chat. A long time ago, in self-preservation, he'd become closed and self-sufficient, but Madalyn had him wanting small talk.

Madalyn obviously had no idea her posture, pitched slightly forward, gave him the most enchanting glimpse of her cleavage. Her dress was perfectly proper—a shirtwaist with short sleeves and a full skirt, topped by a navy blazer—but with the blazer carefully folded on the seat beside her, the gentle cowling in the neckline of her dress gave him a tantalizing peak of soft white skin.

He shut his eyes briefly and took a long, slow

breath. This adolescent ogling had to stop. This instant. He was being a cad and his behavior was unacceptable. He was acting as though he was starving for female attention when that was hardly the case. If he had been too busy lately to pursue a social life, that hardly meant he was a sex-starved madman. He had control. He was always in control, he tried to assure himself.

When he opened his eyes, he was grateful the flight attendant was standing in the aisle.

"Can I get you anything, sir? Ma'am?"

"Ice water with lemon for me. Madalyn?" he asked.

"I'll have the same."

"We have a full selection of drinks and a stocked bar. Are you sure you wouldn't like something else?" Philip asked, not wanting her to be shy.

"No, really. Water is fine."

As the attendant disappeared behind the curtain, he couldn't resist the urge to tease her. "Are you sure? I promise not to tell the boss if you spill something."

She flushed beet-red. "Am I being that obvious?"

"No, not at all," he said kindly, relenting at her obvious distress.

"Liar," she said, her lips quirking wryly. She immediately clamped her hand over her mouth, her flush receding and her eyes going huge as she realized what she'd just said.

Philip barked a laugh. "It's all right, Madalyn. I really do have a sense of humor, you know."

She looked away as a blush crept up her neck again. "Actually, I don't know that. I'm just so unbalanced right now. Everything has happened so fast. I—I can't seem to get my brain to sort it all out yet. I mean, in barely over a day, I've gotten a job I've only dreamed about, had a limo ride, and now I'm off on a private jet to a business meeting. If I didn't know better, I'd think I was dreaming.''

"I admit this isn't my usual modus operandi. Things are a bit off-kilter for me, as well."

"But I'm sure you don't feel like a toddler in church, waiting to be told to sit still and keep quiet."

When their drinks arrived, Philip accepted his glass with a nod of thanks. He waited until Madalyn had taken a long, almost desperate drink before he caught her eye.

"I promise not to scold, Madalyn. You can relax."

"Oh, I doubt that," she said, her humor returning. "But I promise I'll try."

Philip returned to his notes, and Madalyn hid a sigh of relief. He really was being nice. She felt like such a bumpkin, but had decided from the start it would have been ridiculous to pretend she was used to such luxury. Nothing in her day-to-day struggle to keep her head above water could possibly have prepared her for this absolute decadence. She could never have pulled off nonchalance so she'd been up-front about how she felt, but for a moment she'd wished she had the experience and sophistication to appear undaunted.

Not to mention that having nothing to do was playing havoc with her already taut nerves. He probably thought he was being nice to refrain from dictating, or giving her something to type. Instead she was left with a magazine that held no interest, and watching his face as he concentrated—which held great interest. She tried and tried to tell herself he was just a boss, like any old boss, and to quit acting like a ninny.

But he was hardly "any old boss" and her hormones knew it.

Surely she could be forgiven a moment of fantasy, she reasoned, when surrounded by such opulence. After all, she might work in the city, but she was still a small-town girl at heart. And her mother had meant well, but Madalyn was still plagued now and again by those knight-in-shining-armor thoughts, only this knight's castle was hundreds of stories high, and his destrier had shiny white wings and landing gear.

With the flight less than two hours long, in no time it seemed they were walking down the carpeted halls of an older but exceptionally restored hotel. The clerk behind the front desk had swiftly given Philip the key to his family's suite, and handed her a key to the smaller suite directly across the hall. Philip mentioned on the elevator ride up that the top floor was always reserved for his family so she didn't have to worry about noisy neighbors.

Madalyn barely refrained from shaking her head in amazement. She had stayed at a hotel of this calibre only a few times before, for conferences she'd attended, but she'd always had the cheapest room she could manage, and even then at conference rates. While she realized the Ambercrofts probably didn't give room rates a second thought, she still could hardly imagine having an entire floor at one's disposal.

Just one more eye-popper to add to her growing list.

Philip left her at the door to her room, telling her to relax for a couple of hours before they met the McConnallys downstairs for drinks and dinner. He pointed out there was a private pool and hot tub on the roof, if she was interested in a swim, and she was grateful she'd given in to the whim to throw her swimsuit into her bag.

The room was simply too quiet when Philip left, and there was nothing on the television worth wasting her time on. A swim sounded wonderful, and maybe a few minutes in the hot tub would relax her. She felt so tense, she wondered why her elbows didn't meet behind her back.

It didn't take but a minute to strip out of her jacket and dress, and into the modest maillot she'd had for several years. She'd chosen the classic style for its durability, and combined with the fact that she rarely had the opportunity to go swimming, it looked almost new. She felt silly for being self-conscious about her less-than-flat tummy when Philip wouldn't even see her, but she couldn't help it.

The roof was empty when she stepped out into the sunshine, and she took a moment to enjoy the view of the gulf from behind the Plexiglas barrier keeping the brisk wind away. A dip of her toe in the pool assured her it was heated—again no surprise—and with a sigh she slipped off the robe she'd taken from her room and dove in.

She lost track of time as she swam laps, enjoying the gentle pull of her muscles as she exercised. The pull also reminded her that hefting a twenty-month-old did not constitute real exercise, and that she needed to put some back in her schedule.

The question was: When? She worked all day, and she certainly didn't want to give up any of her precious evening time with her baby. Maybe it was time to invest in some aerobics tapes she could work out to when the little darling was down for the night. Except, realistically, she was always exhausted by then and ready for her own "night-nights."

Madalyn switched from the pool to the hot tub and relaxed her back against the stainless-steel side. She didn't dare give in to "what ifs." What if she had even a portion of this kind of wealth and didn't have to work? What if she could give her child all the things she should have by rights, if her father wasn't a scum-sucking worm? What if...?

No, she'd just said she wouldn't indulge in "what ifs," hadn't she? What had happened, happened, and there was no going back. Hindsight was twenty-twenty, although she consoled herself that the worm had well hidden his scum-sucking nature. She still had moments when she blamed herself for being deceived, but the majority of the time she was at peace herself.

She forced herself to relax, letting the effervescent bubbles work their magic. She was a good judge of character, notwithstanding her one monumental mistake. And she could never consider the experience totally without merit since she had her precious Erin. And, if she were looking for silver linings, even tarnished ones, she could count that she was older and wiser now. If anything, it had proven to her that she could be self-sufficient, and had once and for all cured any remaining dreams of knights coming to rescue her. Very rich, handsome knights.

She might not have it all, but she had what mattered. And while she was content to take care of herself and her child, if the right guy happened along some day—some nice, middle-class, hardworking, average-looking guy—then that would be fine. Someone she would be content with, someone she could care for. Blazing passion and overwhelming love were things she could do without, thank you very much. She'd been burned once, and overwhelmed once, and it was too painful a process to even consider repeating.

Her traitorous mind immediately asked her what it might be like to have a man like Philip desire her. At the least he radiated energy, and she had little trouble imagining that energy being applied to his lovemaking. He went after everything with a passion and single-mindedness that had her breathing a bit faster when she considered what that would mean in the bedroom.

She stood abruptly and headed for the ladder. This had to stop. The sensuality of warm water bubbling over her skin had obviously bubbled her brain, as well. With a determined huff, she toweled off and slipped her robe over her shoulders. She didn't meet Philip in the hallway back to her room, so she assumed he was hard at work in his suite. Thankfully. The last thing she needed was to see him.

A cool shower, and re-dressing, took up the last of

her precious two hours. When Philip called, she was ready to go in her one and only cocktail dress, her good black pumps and her serviceable clutch. She was no Neiman-Marcus mannequin, but she wasn't ashamed of herself, either.

Philip, on the other hand, had changed into a linen suit with his crisp white shirt open at the neck. She resisted the urge to tell him he wasn't fooling anyone. He might be trying to appear casual, but there was nothing casual about him. That energy she'd noticed was in high gear, and she wondered if he shorted electrical equipment when he walked by. The look he was giving her was certainly doing a number on *her* electrical systems.

It was a relief to meet the McConnallys and have Philip's magnetism deflected. Mrs. McConnally was obviously charmed, and Mr. McConnally had his own portion of charm himself. All in all, it made their predinner drinks in the bar attached to the four-star restaurant an amusing, pleasant icebreaker.

Over dinner the men discussed business lightly, and Madalyn was delighted to see Mr. McConnally not only solicit comments from his wife, but genuinely listen to her answers. It made Madalyn inexplicably happy that these people were no pushovers. Maybe she was projecting, but she couldn't help but think about the Prices, and the dilemma they currently faced. When they made the decision to sell or not, she wanted them to be on an equal footing, much like the McConnallys were. Unfortunately she knew that was unrealistic in the Prices' situation. She just wished she could do something—anything—to help them.

Focusing back on the conversation, she let the evening flow around her.

Philip controlled his exuberance with a finely trained hand. The deal was as good as in the bag.

They were standing outside the restaurant, saying their good-nights to the McConnallys. Connar had just shaken his hand and said, ''Let's meet in the mornin' and get this puppy ironed out.''

As the valet brought the car around, and the McConnallys drove away, Philip resisted the urge to grab Madalyn in a fierce hug and plant a kiss on her beautiful lips. He was caught in the rush of excitement that always came with a big win, but even that didn't explain his unusual desire.

It had been bad enough that he could hardly keep his eyes off of her during dinner. He'd always known the little black dress was a feminine weapon, but Madalyn's dress had been enough to set his pulse racing. There wasn't anything intentionally seductive about the dress—scoop neck, A-line, cap sleeve—but on her, gently hugging her curves, drawing attention to her gorgeous legs...well, he'd had to swallow more than usual from his mouth watering.

He hoped the McConnallys hadn't noticed, although he did remember Connar giving him a wink as they'd seated the ladies at the dinner table.

Connar was a good man. Philip was delighted he wanted to stay with the company, even if just for a couple of transition years. And Mrs. McConnally was equally likable. For all his reputation as a shark, Philip genuinely enjoyed the task of revamping a business. Sometimes it worked out that he could keep the original owner involved, sometimes not, but in this instance, it looked like a happy-all-around situation.

Maybe it was his own longing for a family, a longing he kept deeply buried, that slipped through at moments like these. He knew damn good and well that he was never going to have the happy little nuclear family. That wasn't in his cards. Even if he did settle down and get married, he doubted he could ever be the at-home-by-six kind of guy.

"Well, that went well," Madalyn said, breaking into his thoughts.

"Yes, it did. Thank you."

She looked startled. "What for?"

"For being a delightful dinner companion. I think you won over the McConnallys."

She shook her head. "I hardly think so. Although it was fun to talk babies with Mrs. McConnally. Did you know they have seven grandchildren?"

Did he know that? He couldn't remember. He was having a hard time remembering anything at the moment. He was too busy thinking about how her hair would look if he took the two long sticks that looked like painted chopsticks out of the twist of burnished curls. It was a decidedly unemployerlike thing to do, but he figured wondering couldn't hurt.

"...and their youngest just turned two. That is such a cute age."

Having totally missed what she had been saying, he took the safe road. "So I've heard."

The elevator slid to a smooth stop, and he was curiously bereft at the thought of her going to her room, and him being alone. Against all sane judgment, he found himself saying, "Would you come in for a nightcap, or coffee?"

She hesitated visibly, and he knew he should let her off the hook, but dammit, he was in a great mood and he wanted to share it with someone.

Finally she gave him a nod. "Um, sure. That sounds nice."

He held open his door and ushered her inside. He moved past her to pull open the curtains and then headed for the bar.

Madalyn was drawn to the view before her much as she had been on the roof. The huge plates of glass opened onto a long balcony. The brisk wind off the gulf fluttered the fringes of the canopy over the table, and even though she knew it would be cool, she couldn't resist the urge to go outside.

"May I?" she asked, indicating the sliding door with her hand.

"Certainly. What can I bring you?"

She opted for some seltzer with a twist, deciding the drinks she'd had before dinner had been plenty. When he joined her a moment later, she was leaning against the railing and watching the ocean chase itself onto the curved beach below.

"I don't think I ever get tired of the ocean," she said in a tone a bit dreamy. "Maybe it's because I don't get near it often enough."

Philip shrugged out of his jacket and slipped it around her shoulders. She pulled the lapels together and smiled her thanks even though her equilibrium would have been better served by the bite of the wind. Instead, her senses were being seduced by his warmth held captive in the silky lining caressing her arms and shoulders, and the soft scent of his cologne clinging to the collar.

She accepted her glass and held on for dear life as he leaned with her on the cold bar.

"You really enjoy this, don't you?" she asked, feeling his sense of satisfaction, his pure contentment with the moment.

"It's what makes it all worth it," he answered, obviously aware she wasn't talking about the ocean.

"Winning?"

"Not exactly. I mean, that's part of it, but it's about the whole game, and despite my reputation, it's about knowing good things are happening for the other guy, too." He laughed, a decidedly self-deprecating snort. "Not that I'm totally altruistic, mind you."

For an instant, she thought about talking to him about the Prices. Maybe he could offer some suggestions. But just as quickly she squelched the temptation. She would have to talk to Mr. Price first, at the very least. She'd never betray his confidence, no matter how well-intentioned she might be.

"I can't tell you the last time I was out here," he commented suddenly, watching a boat coming in to dock at the pier off to the left.

She looked at him, stunned that he was completely

serious. "You have your own hotel, on the ocean, and you never come out here?"

"Not here to the hotel, here on the balcony."

"That's even worse! Shame on you," she teased.

He chuckled. "You're right. But at least I can blame you for my current inexplicable behavior."

"I beg your pardon!"

He cut her a grin. "I'm serious. I keep trying to get a handle on the last two days, and it just leaves my head spinning. I can't explain running my mouth more in the last forty-eight hours than I ever have in my life, and I don't think my pulse has slowed down since the moment I met you."

Madalyn knew her eyes were wide in amazement. Her jaw worked, but no sound came out of her throat. How in the world was she supposed to respond to that?

"Madalyn," Philip said softly, studying his hands clasped together in front of him, "I've decided I need to kiss you. It's becoming almost an obsession, and we just need to get it out of the way so things can get back to center."

He turned to her and used the lapels of his coat to gently tug her closer.

"You understand, don't you?"

She nodded first, then shook her head. "Philip, I—"

It was too late. His mouth descended to hers, capturing her completely. And stunning her senseless.

She hadn't been prepared, in her wildest fantasy, for what kissing Philip was really like. His lips were warm and smooth, his tongue an electric jolt as he stroked the corner of her mouth. She opened to him in a gasp, unable to stop even if she had wanted to, and she knew she should…stop.…

She wasn't sure who moaned, but it didn't really matter. Not with the world spinning wildly, forcing her to clutch his shirt to keep from falling. Not with her heart pounding, pressed against his chest, in a rhythm that matched the mad pace of his. Not with the rushing in her ears that couldn't be blamed on the surf below.

Somehow the sticks holding her twist in place disappeared. She didn't remember his hands moving, but now they were buried in her hair.

And this time she was sure he was the one who moaned.

His lips trailed fire down her throat, leaving her breathless as he nipped at the madly pulsing vein on the side of her neck. She wove her fingers through his hair, pulling him closer, needing him closer.

Something, somehow, got through to her fogged brain. She gasped, not merely from the feel of Philip's lips against her bare shoulder, but from the realization that Philip's lips *were* against her bare shoulder.

With one tiny vestige of sanity, she tore herself away, feeling a wrenching ache at the loss of his touch but ignoring the agonizing sensation.

"Philip, I—"

"Madalyn, I'm so sorry."

She did not doubt him. The look on his face showed his own confusion over what had just happened.

He turned away and grabbed the railing. The wind,

cold and brisk, made her shiver with the loss of his jacket, now crumpled on the ground.

She backed toward the glass door he had left open. "I—I'd better go."

He merely nodded and with what little breath she could manage, she hurried across the room and out the door. Her fingers trembled, the least of which from cold, as she tried to key her own door. It took two tries and three curses to get it open, and finally she was safely inside.

In stilted steps, she made it to the bed and jerked back the comforter to topple onto the mattress. She barely managed to haul the covers over her shoulders before the shivers began.

Chapter Five

Philip wasn't sure how Madalyn was going to act when they met for breakfast the next morning. She was still an unknown quantity, as they had hardly known each other long enough for him to form a firm opinion.

But it seemed he'd known her long enough to turn into a total idiot.

Quelling any reminders of what had happened on the balcony, he concentrated on establishing the ground rules to get through the day. It seemed, however, that Madalyn was far ahead of him. Before he knew it, they were well into the meeting and neither one of them had even so much as hinted about last night. They worked together coolly, efficiently. By the time they had wrapped up a successful agreement with McConnally and his attorney, and were in the airplane and returning to Dallas, he had dictated four memos and three letters.

Well, maybe this is going to work out after all. He relaxed into his seat and took his lunch tray from the flight attendant. They had left directly from the meeting, as both of them were anxious to get back. Not that Madalyn had said anything, except to mention her baby and how glad she would be to be home.

So, he concluded, that was that. He had no explanation for the moment of pure madness, but they both obviously accepted that it was over and forgotten. He steadfastly refused to acknowledge the little twinge of disappointment that she seemed to have forgotten the kiss so easily. This was much better than a scene or any rehashing of the event.

Madalyn was the picture of the perfect secretary once again, primly setting aside her notepad to pick up her lunch, her legs neatly crossed. Not a hair out of place.

He thought of the painted chopsticks he'd picked up when he'd finally pried his fingers from the cold railing. He'd put them in his briefcase and planned on returning them to her later. Now certainly wasn't the time for reminders. He knew they weren't valuable in a strictly monetary sense, but had no idea if they had sentimental worth.

"Tell me about your little girl," he said, deciding it was time to get his mind off of last night.

The smile that instantly came to her face told him that he'd chosen the right topic for their luncheon conversation.

"Her name is Erin and she's twenty months old. She has dark brown hair and brown eyes, and has the cutest little dimples."

Philip couldn't help but smile back, and suddenly his perfectly prepared food had taste. He took a sip of fragrant coffee and looked at her over the rim of his cup.

"So what does a twenty-month-old do?"

Madalyn swallowed the bite she'd taken and thought for a moment. "They're perpetual motion machines. She's into everything, and you can't leave her alone for a minute. She delights in finding a cabinet I've forgotten to lock, and I think she considers chase the ultimate game."

"Does she talk?"

Madalyn started to speak, then stopped herself. She cocked her head and gave him a teasing grin. "You're not around children much, are you."

"I notice you said that as a statement, not a question." He chuckled and dug into his chocolate layer cake. "No, I can safely say that children are foreign to me. The next generation of Ambercrofts hasn't started coming along yet, so no nieces and nephews to provide experience."

"Do you want children of your own?"

He started to give the pat answer of "of course," but found himself hesitating. "I'm not sure," he said finally.

Her eyebrow rose in surprise. "Well, that's refreshingly honest!"

He shrugged. "As it appears the continuation of the Ambercroft line is falling on my shoulders, I suppose I'll have to, but I'm not sure that I want to."

"No child should be an obligation," she said softly, but with iron-strong conviction.

"You're right," he answered just as honestly. "That was a stupid thing to say. I apologize."

"Don't apologize. Just don't have children unless you want them. They're precious. I know because I wasn't sure I wanted children. I had to do some serious soul searching when I got pregnant, and it changed my life. But even being a single parent is worth it, at least for me."

Having no point of reference to draw from, he accepted her at her word. "Is Erin's father not in the picture?" he asked, knowing it really wasn't his business. More than curiosity prompted his question, though. He needed to know if there was a man in her life, even a sideline kind of guy.

Her eyes gave away both a sadness and a determination that had him wondering what she was thinking. "No. I made the incredibly stupid mistake of falling in love with my boss a few years ago. Little did I realize at the time that he was all for a fling, but nothing to do with rings. I was fired for—" she made a sour face "—misconduct the day after he learned I was pregnant. So much for the office romance fairy tale."

She said it so casually, he knew she was giving him a direct warning. Funny. What bothered him was not the warning—he probably deserved that. What bothered him was that she had had an experience that caused her to need to warn him in the first place.

"And no," she continued, "that isn't on my résumé. I worked for him for just under a year."

"I noticed you put year-to-year dates on your employment history, but that's quite common now.

Makes it easy to hide a small gap in employment history.''

"I don't really have any gaps in my employment. I went to work for the Prices right away. I was lucky they're such wonderful people. From day one they knew I was pregnant and didn't care. And they love to play surrogate grandparents to Erin at every opportunity."

"This isn't the first time you've spoken so highly of the Prices. I'm surprised you're leaving at all with what you've been saying."

He didn't miss her sharp glance away from him. He consoled his conscience that he wasn't asking her anything unethical. He just wanted to know what had inspired such abiding loyalty.

"I'd work for them forever, but I think I told you Mrs. Price wants to come back. She says she's bored with the charity circuit. Besides, I think they're considering…um…retiring soon, and they've probably got plans I'm not privy to."

Philip took the hint and let the subject drop as their trays were taken away. It seemed logical, with lunch over, to get back to work. He decided that they had enough "sharing" for his comfort level for one day…even if he had been the one to choose the topic.

After the plane touched down, the limo took Madalyn back home. Philip let her take off what little was left of the afternoon, more for his sake than for hers, but she didn't need to know that.

But, somehow, the office felt lonely. In fifteen years his office had never felt lonely.

How odd….

* * *

Madalyn didn't argue with Philip about staying home. Most of the day was gone, and she nearly tripped over herself hurrying inside to see her baby. She'd thought one night away wouldn't be a big deal, but it had been.

After a nice dinner and a long talk with her mother, Madalyn got Erin ready for bed and then snuggled her close as they settled into her favorite chair in the nursery. While Erin was immediately soothed by the gentle rocking, it took quite a bit longer for Madalyn's mind to settle.

She placed a kiss on the downy soft hair on the back of Erin's head.

"You know," she whispered conversationally, "in a very odd way I'm glad this happened. Now Mommy can stop being such a ninny."

Madalyn rubbed soft circles on Erin's back. She was sound asleep and could be put down in the bed, but tonight Mommy needed this together time more than Baby did.

"You see," she continued whispering to her inattentive audience, "now Mommy can put her little fantasy to rest. She's kissed him and they both know what a monumental mistake it was. Although, I have to tell you, he's one incredibly good kisser."

Mistake was probably a giant misnomer. Madalyn couldn't even think of a word big enough to describe how huge the mistake had been. At least they both had instantly recognized it and things were back on an even keel. They were both mature enough to get past it and continue working as the professionals they were. He had even taken her warning on the plane earlier with good grace.

Except for the tiny part that wished he'd been as devastated by the kiss as she had been, the rest of her was extremely glad everything she was working for had not been destroyed. She liked this job, and would be devastated if she got fired.

Or if she had to quit. At least it looked now as though that wasn't going to be necessary. That ridiculous kiss had at least served to jerk her out of the little fantasy she hadn't even realized she'd slipped into—the old, old one about knights and white horses and living happily ever after. With the effectiveness of an electric-shock treatment, she was now wired to the fact that Philip was the boss, she was the secretary, and never the lines would be crossed again.

She steadfastly ignored the little ache in her heart that thought brought.

"Besides, he doesn't even know if he wants children." She kissed Erin's head again. "Stupid man."

Erin gave one of the sweet baby sighs that always made Madalyn melt with happiness, and she took it as a sign of her daughter's brilliant agreement.

"You're right, we don't need him. We don't need anybody. This is just a job. That's all."

When she finally relinquished her sleeping child to her crib, she decided not to mention to Erin that her mother had just told a whopping lie.

At breakfast, Erin didn't seem to notice that her mother's eyes were red-rimmed from another night of little sleep. Madalyn was grateful that toddlers weren't capable of asking probing questions, mostly because she didn't want to face the answers. Thankfully the morning routine helped her regain her mental balance. By the time she arrived at work, it felt almost normal to step off the elevator and head for the massive desk now piled with folders. She knew it wasn't hers permanently, but for today it was, and it restored a bit of her equilibrium to dig in and feel efficient and capable once again.

She had half the desk cleared by the time the elevator doors opened again. She didn't even look up as she was sure it was Philip. He'd offer his customary good morning greeting as he walked by and into his office.

Instead, she nearly jumped out of her seat when a body skirted her peripheral vision and sat down on the edge of her desk.

"Halloo," an amused male voice said as she swiveled her chair around. "Definitely not Mrs. Montague, so I'm guessing...hmm...Miss Moneypenny?"

Madalyn didn't need a brick to fall on her to realize this was Gene Ambercroft. Even if she didn't recognize him from the many times she'd seen him in one magazine or another, he was instantly identifiable as an Ambercroft from the dark hair—although not as dark as Philip's, and the aquiline features—though not as handsome as Philip's, and the tanned, muscular body—although not as breathtaking as Philip's.

Madalyn smiled and held out her hand. "Hello, I'm Madalyn Wier. And you must be Gene."

He grinned in return, and held her hand much longer than necessary. "Must I be?" He sighed. "I guess I must."

Madalyn chuckled and disengaged her hand with a minimum of struggle. "Mrs. Montague is on vacation. I'm filling in."

"Lucky Bond...I mean, Philip."

There was something so instantly charming about the man that Madalyn just couldn't make herself put on the prim-and-proper act. She could easily see how his reputation had burgeoned as the playboy cowboy, as he was often tagged in the press. If he was this suave teasing a secretary, she could only imagine the effect he had when really putting on the charm.

But as to Bond...er...Philip, she wasn't so sure he was lucky, so she didn't respond. Instead she said, "Philip isn't in yet. Shall I tell him you stopped by?"

"He's not in yet?" Gene put his hand to his chest as though his heart was failing. "Quick, call an ambulance. He must be sick or dying or something."

A snort came from the direction of the elevator doors. "Or something," Philip said, moving across the room. He glanced at Madalyn. "Cancel the ambulance."

She fought a smile, unsuccessfully, as she nodded.

"Morning, brother. Sleeping in?"

Philip's smile was strained. "Some of us have things like, oh, meetings with boards of directors, which means our day starts generally before brunch."

Gene clutched his chest again and looked at Madalyn. "Call the ambulance back. *I'm* the one who's wounded."

Philip obviously saw his own pomposity and rolled his eyes. He shook his brother's offered hand and slapped him on the shoulder.

"I didn't know you were back. How was Europe?" he asked with what Madalyn thought was sincere curiosity.

"Did you miss me? And Europe is cold." Gene returned the affectionate slap and caught Madalyn's attention. "Take a note, darling. Never, ever let me go to England before July again. March is still the dead of winter there. I forget, living in Texas."

Madalyn grabbed a notepad and began writing furiously. "Got it."

Gene burst out laughing. "Hey, Philip, I like her. Can I have her?"

"She's not a puppy, Gene. And no, you can't."

"But you've got the battle-ax—I mean, Mrs. Montague—who keeps you running like a top. Can't you see I need the efficient Ms. Wier to put me in order?"

Philip grabbed Gene by the front of his shirt and began dragging him toward the office. "Forget it, or I'll personally take care of putting you *in* an order. How do you feel about the Franciscans?"

Gene cast a pleading glace over his shoulder and mouthed, "Help me!"

Madalyn released a giggle when the door finally closed between her and the two brothers.

The mere thought of Gene and monks in the same sentence was enough to bring on another fit of laughter, and it took a determined application of discipline and burying herself back in her tasks to sober up.

She squelched any curiosity when she heard raised voices from the inner sanctum. She couldn't hear distinct words, of course, and she wasn't trying to listen. It was even more difficult not to be curious when laughter filtered through sometime later. It seemed from first appearances that the brothers were truly brothers—fighting one minute, laughing the next. Not that she'd know, being female and an only child, but that was the impression she had.

She also had a feeling of gratitude that she was working for Philip. She had taken an instant liking to Gene, but she loved being in the thick of things working for Philip. Even though she was aware that she was not being given sensitive material and files, she was given so many things to do that she was never bored.

With the exception of saying goodbye when the men left for lunch together, Madalyn didn't have a chance to speak with Gene again. It seemed Philip was hurrying Gene out, but Madalyn decided that was silly. With a shrug, she went back to work.

The rest of the day went so smoothly, she was almost afraid to trust it. She had been ignoring the nagging fear that things were still going to fall apart due to what she now referred to as the moment of temporary insanity.

When the rest of the week went by with equal equilibrium, she started to breathe a bit easier. Philip appeared pleased with her work, and as he seemed as firmly committed to pretending the balcony scene hadn't happened, she was confident that her place at Ambercroft, Inc., was secure. She and Philip had established a rhythm that worked flawlessly, and they had managed to transition back to being comfortable with each other. Being busy helped, and she gained a new respect for how much work it took to manage the many holdings of Ambercroft, Inc. But she loved the job, hectic pace and all, and was going to hate it when Mrs. Montague returned.

Her mother went back to Louisiana on Saturday, and by Sunday afternoon, she and Erin were firmly back in their routine.

It seemed too good to be true, yet the next week started out just as smoothly.

She should have known it was the calm before the storm.

In the wee hours of the morning on Wednesday, she came awake with a panic to Erin's anguished cries. Madalyn knew the instant she picked Erin up that she had a fever, and a high one.

It was an automatic response to go into her Dr. Mom role. The thermometer said Erin's fever was high, but not dangerous, and the next obvious step was to give her a dose of medicine to bring the fever down, bathe her and then change the damp sheets in the crib. Erin didn't want to be put down even for those few minutes, but Madalyn keep crooning to her and got the work done. Then they settled into the rocker, Erin with a bottle of electrolyte solution made just for children when they're sick, and Madalyn with a cup of strong coffee.

This was hardly the first time they'd gone through this. Erin had struggled with chronic ear infections, but it had looked like the cycle had been broken. Madalyn was fairly sure this was another infection— all the classic symptoms were the same. The fever, Erin pulling at her ear, the toddler's inability to sleep for more than a catnap's worth...

It was going to be a long night.

Madalyn jerked awake a few hours later, stunned to see bright sunlight streaming through the crack in Erin's curtains. A bleary glance at the clock near the changing table informed her it was just after eight o'clock.

She carefully placed the sleeping Erin in her crib, doubtful but hopeful that the poor sweetheart would stay down for a few minutes while Madalyn called the doctor and Philip.

The pediatrician's office finally answered, and Madalyn set up an appointment, although she wondered why, when it never failed that she ended up waiting what seemed like forever to see the doctor.

Her call to Philip came next. She dreaded it as she dialed the office and was put through. Erin came first, but Madalyn was struck with an intense sadness that this probably meant she was going to lose this job. It was a temp position anyway, and bosses weren't known for their patience with permanent employees when the kids got in the way. It was the kiss of death for a temp to have to take off.

For half a second, she wished she'd get his voice mail, but then chided herself for being chicken. Besides, the chances of him not being in the office were slim and—

"Philip Ambercroft."

"Philip, this is Madalyn. I'm sorry I'm not in."

"Are you all right?"

The worry she detected made her feel guilty that she'd fallen asleep with Erin and was so late in calling. "I'm fine, but my child is sick. I've got to take

her to the pediatrician's office at ten-thirty so I won't
be in today. I'm very sorry.''

"That's all right.''

"I understand if you need to seek another temp—''

"That won't be necessary. Just let me know how
things are going, will you?''

"Certainly. And thank you.''

The rest of the morning was hectic with a fretting
child who didn't want to be put down, trying to get
herself dressed and making it to the appointment. By
the time they saw the doctor, went to the pharmacy
for antibiotics and got back home, Madalyn was feeling as frustrated as Erin.

Madalyn rarely indulged in self-pity. She had chosen this path, and just as she refused to berate herself
for her mistake in thinking she had loved Erin's father—and even more for thinking that he had loved
her—she refused to whine when things got rough. But
sometimes, just for brief moments, she couldn't stop
an ache of loneliness from catching her by surprise.

She stood by Erin's crib and watched her child,
finally resting peacefully. Tears welled in Madalyn's
eyes and she dashed them away. These were times
she wondered if she was doing the right thing. This
was when she wished she had someone to talk to, to
lean on, for just a moment. She wished she could give
Erin a father who loved her as she deserved to be
loved, a man who wanted to be involved in her life,
to watch her grow and change.

Oh, she could call Keith back home, but that
wouldn't be fair. He had read too much into their one
and only date so it would be cruel to let him think

there was hope for more. Keith was a dear, and Madalyn knew he thought he was in love with her, but she'd yet to convince him that they couldn't be more than friends. He would marry her in a heartbeat, and he adored Erin, which made it all the more sad that Madalyn's heart wouldn't cooperate and return the feelings Keith made so clear. Still, it was tempting when she felt like this, to call.

But just as she couldn't force the man who had helped create Erin to take responsibility for her, Madalyn couldn't marry someone just to ease the burden of single parenthood.

With a deep breath, she straightened her shoulders and made herself put those thoughts behind her. Things were as they were and—

The doorbell rang, interrupting the beginning of her motivational speech. She raced across the house, hoping to get there before the person on the other side of the door rang the bell again and woke Erin up. In her rush to get Erin down, she'd forgotten to put out her Baby Sleeping sign.

Instead of the mailman, who was the only person Madalyn could think of who might be waiting, she found Philip. She stood there, holding the door open, stunned.

"Um, hello," she finally managed, and remembered her manners enough to invite him in.

She noticed his quick glance around her living room before he looked back at her, giving the definite impression that he was uncomfortable. She had to smile, though, when he thrust a bouquet of spring flowers at her, and a pink bunny a half second later.

"Those are for you. To be honest, I wasn't sure what to bring."

"Thank you. I've always wanted a pink bunny."

He thawed a bit and laughed with her. "Actually, that's for your little girl. I wasn't sure what to bring her, either."

"You didn't have to bring anything, Philip, but thank you." She led the way into the kitchen, and after getting them both something to drink, busied herself at the counter arranging the flowers in a vase.

His discomfort was so endearing. She'd never seen him out of command and it was revelatory, but she didn't want to be charmed by him. Respect was fine; even a little awe was good. Those feelings kept distance between them. Charm, however, made her go warm inside, made her want to hug him, laugh with him. Those were dangerous thoughts.

"Is something wrong?" she asked, hoping to tactfully find out why he was there. Good news or bad, she'd rather have it up front.

"Wrong?"

She shrugged. "I'm trying to figure out why you'd drive all the way out here."

His laugh was self-deprecating. "To be honest, I'm not sure, either. I was sitting in my office after you called and I began thinking about you being a single parent and what it must be like to have a sick child. I know from your call that you're worried about your job, and I decided I needed to let you know that everything's okay. I tried to call, but I assume you were at the doctor's or whatever, and I just gave in to the impulse to drive over and check on you."

She listened to his short speech with nothing short of amazement. Even Mr. and Mrs. Price had never checked on her personally when things like this happened. They always called, but had never come over. This was definitely a first.

"I don't know what to say, except thank you. Erin and I are fine."

She put the finished vase on the table and was left with nothing to do with her hands. She thrust them into the pocket of her shorts to keep from fidgeting. It only reminded her of how she looked, and she was suddenly self-conscious. Her hair was pulled back in a ponytail, her tank top had seen better days even before Erin had drooled on it and her shorts were designed for comfort, not fashion. She had on no makeup, no jewelry and no shoes.

All in all, she felt completely self-conscious in front of her impeccably dressed boss.

He didn't seem to notice her discomfort. He seemed caught in his own frustration, and she assumed it was because they didn't have a lot to talk about—which was just one more nail in the coffin of her momentary fantasies about Philip. Having him in her little three-bedroom home was a forceful, even a little painful, illustration of just how far apart their worlds were.

Erin woke up and Madalyn excused herself to go rescue the tyke from her crib. Her little face was still a bit flushed, but the fever was down.

"Is she all right?" Philip asked worriedly from the doorway of the baby's room.

"She's going to be fine," Madalyn assured him,

arranging a receiving blanket over her shoulder for the baby to lay her head on.

"Erin," she said, "this is Mommy's boss. Can you say hello?"

Erin shook her head against Madalyn's shoulder and she smiled softly at Philip. "She gets shy sometimes. I'm sorry."

"Don't apologize. I wasn't expecting an introduction, to be honest."

"Her fever is down, and the medicine should kick in soon. Then she'll be her usual gregarious self. She has an ear infection, which isn't contagious, but I'm not comfortable leaving her with the sitter when she's this fussy."

Philip seemed shocked. "Did I say something to imply I thought you should take her to the sitter? I meant what I said about it being fine that you needed to take off from work."

Madalyn felt a tension she hadn't even known was there relax in her shoulders. "You didn't say anything of the sort. I think I was just feeling a little defensive."

Philip scratched the back of his neck. "I'm thinking my impulsive drive over wasn't such a good move. I seem to have made you uncomfortable instead of reassured."

She led the way back into the living room. "Please don't feel that way. It was really sweet of you."

She had taken a seat in what she and Erin called the big rocker, to differentiate it from the wooden rocker in the nursery, and Philip sat on the couch.

"I admit I was worried about losing the job," she

confessed when they were settled. "I would have been sad because I'm having a great time."

"Don't be concerned. I'd be insane to try and find another temp when we work so well together."

"I appreciate that. It's just surprising to find you so understanding."

"Me personally, or in general?"

She blushed, feeling her cheeks heat as red as Erin's. "A man in your position," she amended diplomatically. "You're not only being generous, you're letting me take up a lot of your time."

She had given him the perfect out to make his excuses and leave, but he didn't seem so inclined. He still seemed nervous, which was a picture she wasn't used to, but he also seemed determined—something she was already very used to. Determined to do what, she wasn't sure.

"Will Erin's father check on her?"

The question came out of the blue. After a quick mental review of their conversation on the plane, she realized she'd told him very little about her situation and was astounded at his curiosity.

"No, I don't have any contact with him."

"He doesn't see Erin at all?"

"He doesn't claim her at all."

Philip didn't speak for a moment. "So when you said you were a single parent…"

"I meant it literally. I'm it, the whole enchilada."

"I had no idea."

"Does it matter? Affect my job, I mean?"

"No, not at all. I was just thinking…well, actually, I don't know what I was thinking."

Madalyn hooked her toes on the coffee table and set the rocker in motion again. "Look, Philip, I really appreciate you coming over to check on us, but you don't need to be worried. Erin and I are just fine. Her father has chosen not to be responsible, and I don't want him in her life unless he wants to be."

"You could force him to take responsibility."

Madalyn chuckled. "I could force him to give me money, you mean?"

"It's not right that he has just left you to bear this alone."

Madalyn's smile was sad. "Money isn't the answer to every problem, Philip. Yes, I could take the guy to court and make him pay child support, but you know what? I don't need him, his money or his interference. He chose to trade making child-support payments for signing a termination of his parental rights."

"What a jerk," Philip said vehemently. He looked at Erin and shook his head. "How could he do that?"

"He doesn't want to be bothered is my guess." She gave a short laugh. "I heard he's getting married. To a wealthy socialite, just as I found out he'd always planned. He told me he had plans to be upwardly mobile, and no little bastard was going to keep him from his goals."

"He called Erin that?"

Madalyn nodded.

"What did you say?"

"I didn't say anything. I slugged him and walked out. I haven't ever set eyes on him again."

"I wish I knew what to say."

"There's nothing you need to say, Philip," she assured him, her amusement returning. "Chivalry is indeed dead, and things don't end happily every after. Erin and I will do just fine on our own."

Philip was quiet for so long her curiosity nearly got the better of her common courtesy. Erin brought the needed interruption by wanting down. With a child's ability to bounce back, she was feeling better and wanted to play.

Keeping an eye on Erin, Madalyn said, "I really appreciate the visit and all, but I'm sure you've got to get back to the office."

He took his cue and stood, and she took care not to smile at the sense of relief he tried to hide.

"Yes, I guess I should at that. Is there anything I can do for you before I leave?"

She chuckled, bending over to toss back the toy Erin had thrown. "No, but thank you again. This was a nice surprise."

At the door, Philip snapped his fingers and turned back around. "I nearly forgot. If Erin is feeling all right, remember that tomorrow is our employee day at Six Flags. We'll have child care there, if you can make it."

She remembered the first day she'd worked, she'd typed a memo about the family day that Ambercroft was sponsoring for its employees, but she hadn't even considered that the vacation day would apply to her.

"That's sweet but—"

"Don't say you shouldn't go," he said sternly. "You are an Ambercroft employee and tenure does not matter for this event. In fact, I think I'd better pick you and Erin up."

Madalyn shook her head, fighting an explicable sense of panic. A whole day of fun and sun with Philip? That would be courting disaster. "No, Philip, really."

"Is it because Erin won't feel up to it?" he asked, looking pointedly at the child who was chortling at the toy on the floor in front of her.

"She'll be fine, probably, but—"

"Then that's settled. I'll come by around nine o'clock and we'll be there when the park opens."

"Philip—"

"You're not arguing with the boss again, are you?" he asked with mock severity.

She finally gave in. "No, I'm not arguing. Thank you, once again."

He looked a bit sheepish, cutting her a grin. "Well, I have to confess, I have an ulterior motive."

"And what would that be?" She grinned back, holding on to the door to bolster her wobbly knees. When he smiled like that she couldn't seem to stop her palms from sweating and her heart from racing. She also couldn't resist the invitation to flirt back.

"I hate feeling like a third wheel at these things."

His answer took her totally by surprise. "Pardon?"

"I'm the boss. Everyone expects me to be there, but no one is really comfortable with me. So if I had a date of my own, it might actually be fun."

"A date?"

"Yeah, you know, someone to ride the rides with, eat cotton candy, the whole shebang."

"But surely—"

"Nope, I've made up my mind. I'll see you tomorrow morning."

A wail from Erin forced Madalyn to say a quick goodbye and hurry to tend to her toddler. It was nothing more serious than a momentary frustration with a toy, but Philip was gone....

Leaving Madalyn wondering just what in the world she'd gotten herself into.

Philip drove back downtown wondering just what in the world he'd done, and why! At the moment it had seemed like such a good idea, the only good idea he'd had the whole day.

When he'd arrived at Madalyn's, he'd felt like a fool. But with her usual good humor, she'd made him feel at ease again.

Well, as much as possible considering his reaction to seeing her in shorts and a tank top. He didn't know what he was expecting, but it hadn't been the slightly harried but sexy as hell package she'd presented. She always wore her hair so perfectly contained, and her suits were so perfectly proper, he hadn't been ready for the luscious expanse of leg the shorts had revealed, nor the delicious cleavage the scoop neck of her top displayed. He'd tried not to be a total boor and stare, but he'd been uncomfortably aware of his body's reaction from the moment she'd opened the door.

And her house had taken him by surprise, as well. She was the ideal secretary—cool, efficient, organized. Her lawn had been just as he'd expected, neatly cut with flower beds just beginning to bloom. He'd been impressed, especially now that he knew she didn't have anyone to help her. She had a real talent for design, though how she got it all done was beyond him.

But when she'd invited him inside, he'd stopped in his tracks. A solid blue couch was covered with brilliant pillows. A huge poster of van Gogh's sunflowers took the wall above the fireplace mantel. A welded Kokopelli danced with his flute on one wall, while a Georgia O'Keeffe flower took up most of another. Under normal circumstances, nothing would have gone together, but somehow Madalyn had made it work. It was eclectic, colorful and eye-catching. And nothing like what he'd expected. Her kitchen had been done in a strawberry theme, from canisters to curtains to hand towels. The baby's room had been a nursery rhyme motif, and he thought he'd caught Humpty Dumpty and the Cat and the Fiddle, but the rest had been lost on him.

Still not sure why he'd gone over personally in the first place, he'd been uncomfortable with this side of her. Maybe it was a good thing he'd come after all. It made him see how different they were, how different their life-styles were. Unfortunately it only made worse this nagging urge in him that wanted to take care of her.

Despite her obvious independence, despite the fact that she was an employee—nothing more, nothing less—he couldn't seem to get a grip on this desire to get to know her. He'd never asked Mrs. Montague about her kids. Hell, he hadn't asked more than the perfunctory questions about the grandchild she'd gone to see. Yet he was asking Madalyn personal questions about Erin's father!

He pressed his hand to his forehead, wondering if he was the one with the fever....

There was something about knowing how alone she was that wouldn't let him go. Maybe it was some kind of convoluted tie to his own childhood, he didn't know. He loved his father, missed him greatly at times, but Philip Ambercroft III had never been a dad. A father, yes. A dad, no. And that was one of the things Philip suddenly realized he wanted when he married—to be a dad.

And watching Madalyn handle Erin had made all those urges he thought he had suppressed come surging forward. Erin was an adorable little girl, with her mother's features and dark hair. She'd smiled at him, finally, with her head tucked under Madalyn's chin. Madalyn hadn't even seen it, but he had, and his heart had been captured.

He wasn't around children much. Truth be told, he wasn't around them at all. He didn't know what he was supposed to do, so he just smiled back and then she'd wriggled down from Madalyn's lap and had gone to play.

The invitation to go with him to the company picnic had been as much of a surprise to him as it had obviously been to Madalyn. But it had made sense at the time. He really did feel like a third wheel at these kinds of things, which would probably surprise most people. He knew everyone saw him as this kind of distant entity, not a "real" employee like them, which in one sense was true. Yet they would think him cold if he didn't show up. It made for a tremendous Catch-22.

Having someone to walk around with who wouldn't be on guard since they were with "the boss" had suddenly seemed like a great idea. Madalyn hadn't exhibited any fear of him from day one, something he liked tremendously, so at the time it had made sense to make her his date for the day.

It wasn't until just now, as he was alone again and driving, that he realized what he'd asked. They had worked diligently to distance themselves from each other since that evening on the balcony. He could still recall every instant of that kiss with crystal clarity, and that was dangerous. Back at the office she'd been safe behind her role as secretary and his as boss, and now he'd put them in a dangerous situation again. All because he'd let his usual discipline slip. He had never given in to loneliness before, and he might end up paying a high price for the indulgence. It was risky opening doors he had firmly shut a long time ago, doors he'd been sure were permanently sealed.

He pulled into his parking space and shut off the engine. They would just have to make the best of it. If they were lucky, they'd end up enjoying the day with no damage.

If they were lucky.

Chapter Six

Madalyn knew the instant she saw him at the door that the whole idea was a terrible mistake. Nothing could have prepared her for the effect of Philip Ambercroft in navy shorts, a white polo shirt and a golf cap. He looked so...accessible. She had started to think *normal,* but there was nothing normal or ordinary about him. If his broad shoulders, narrow waist and long legs had been a boon to the suit industry, then those assets were a God-given gift to women when he supported the sportswear industry.

When she finally recovered enough to let him in, she busied herself collecting her hip pack and water bottle, regretting that she had taken Erin to the sitter this morning. The forecast was too windy to take her to the amusement park, and staying in her normal routine was best for Erin anyway. Still, Madalyn regretted not having the buffer an active toddler would have provided.

Not that she needed a buffer, she admonished herself sternly. She was over that silly nonsense for good. She could handle a casual day with the boss. It was no big deal. A piece of cake. A walk in the park.

A giant nightmare...

Determinedly she faced Philip again.

He looked behind her. "I take it your little girl isn't going with us?"

Madalyn snapped her hip pack around her waist. "I thought it would be best if she stayed out of the wind. She was fine this morning, but I didn't want to take any chances."

For just an instant he seemed uncomfortable, and Madalyn wondered if he, too, had been planning on the safety shield Erin's presence would have provided. Then she gave herself a stern mental shake. That was utter nonsense. Philip probably hadn't given a second thought to that kiss, and he was merely being a considerate boss by escorting her to the park. That was it. Pure and simple.

She was running out of clichés.

With a decisive straightening of her shoulders, she followed him out the door. If she could just consider this as sort of an abnormal workday—and keep her eyes off his behind—she might get through it relatively unscathed.

In fact, the day ended up being a mixed dose. The time spent in line visiting with other people turned out to be very pleasant. Even the short duration of the rides themselves was fun. It was during things like the slow train ride around the park that made her short of breath. Philip was so casual about resting his arm on the seat behind her, or putting his hand solicitously on her back. They were the kind of gentlemanly moves she wasn't used to.

Another perfect example being that as she sat under the shade of an oak tree, Philip was standing in line to buy lunch. She couldn't remember the last time someone had waited on her. Just sitting quietly by herself was a luxury she was rarely afforded, much less being treated so royally.

In a paradoxical way, it served to lodge home how alone she was. Her routine helped her keep her mind off of such things, which was one reason her routine never included outings such as this in the first place. She knew Philip had no idea what his ingrained courtesy was doing to her. He'd probably be horrified. Just as she was horrified to admit to herself, in the middle of Six Flags Theme Park, among hundreds of her fellow employees, that she was falling in love with him.

Dammit, she'd tried so hard to prevent this. She had lectured and lectured herself. She'd tried to remain aloof and professional. She'd buried herself in her work and in her home life.

And none of it, not one thing, had worked. Her heart had still blatantly disobeyed and fallen for a man who was absolutely forbidden. And if there was one thing Madalyn was unequivocally certain of, it was that rich bosses didn't marry their secretaries.

Madalyn admitted she would never be a poster child for the new millennium feminist. She fully confessed she wanted the ring, the white picket fence, the dog—the whole package deal. She wanted more children. She wanted to do PTA and car pool and puppet

shows at the library. It wasn't that she didn't enjoy
her career—she did. She loved her work and she
loved being good at it.

But she wanted it all.

She wanted to be a wife as well as a mother. She
wanted a lover to share her bed with who also shared
her life. If all she was interested in was sex, she was
fairly sure she could find someone to oblige her. But
she wanted more than just the physical. And she
wanted it with Philip.

Oh, she most definitely wanted the physical side of
a relationship. If that one kiss was any tiny hint, sex
with him would be beyond imagination. And for an
instant, she wondered if she could enjoy a relationship
with him, knowing it wouldn't be permanent. Then
she immediately vetoed the thought. She would never
survive knowing him, loving him, making love with
him and then having to walk away. It was more than
anyone could ask of her, than she could ask of herself.

It was better all around if she just accepted that she
could never allow one hint of her feelings to show,
and get on with her life. She would enjoy every day
she worked with him, would store up memories and
then shop her résumé around somewhere far, far
away. She'd always wanted to go to California.
Maybe Washington State. Not that there were enough
square miles on the planet to distance her heart, but
she was a logical woman, and had her share of pride.
She had a child to take care of, and her days of fool-
ishness were over. Still, it would be better not to have
to see him in person, even if she would see him in
her dreams every night.

Philip returned just then, carrying a tray full of food and sodas. It put an effective end to her musings, for which she was grateful. Her heart hurt too much to bear any more at the moment.

She put on her game face and managed a laugh. "Are you hungry?" she asked, sweeping her hand toward the burgers, fries and onion rings piled before her. "I think you have enough here for five people."

He looked sheepish. "I have a confession to make. I love junk food."

She cocked her head. "And?"

"And I don't indulge it much. My stomach got the better of me in line."

"Oh ho! So the nigh-onto-perfect Philip Amber-croft the Fourth has a weak spot. This is information I need to tuck away."

He made a face at her. "Very funny. I don't understand why I have this reputation as being made of marble. I'm a normal guy."

Madalyn snorted. "Uh-huh, a normal guy worth about forty billion dollars."

"I am not worth that much."

"Pretty darn close," she muttered, biting into an onion ring. "Look, Philip, it can't be a big surprise to you that you're an icon."

"Actually, I've never given it much thought before."

Her look must have been skeptical.

"I'm serious. This is all your fault."

"Mine?" she said, straightening abruptly. "What do you mean, my fault?"

"Until I met you, I don't think I've spent ten

minutes considering what anyone thought of me. My life revolved around my work and I knew exactly what I was doing. With you, I've babbled away about my family, my childhood, and now you've got me thinking about getting married and having children.''

With someone *suitable,* she thought, her heart twisting even more. Someone on the social register, someone who would enhance the Ambercroft image.

She looked at her food as an excuse to look anywhere but at him.

''Don't blame me for that,'' she finally said after choking down another onion ring. ''If you're thinking about it, it means you were ready to. If I jogged some calcified ideas loose, it was accidental.''

''I was just thinking it was time I—''

Gene chose that moment to whirl over to their table and plop down next to Madalyn. ''Hey, kids, how's it going?'' he interrupted, grabbing an onion ring from Madalyn's plate.

''Hello, Gene,'' she said, pushing her tray over to him in invitation. Let him eat the whole thing, as far as she was concerned. It had all turned to sawdust to her.

''Gene,'' Philip said with a perfunctory nod.

''Am I interrupting?'' he asked with false innocence.

''Yes—''

''No—''

They all laughed, and the tension eased.

''Having fun?'' Madalyn asked, watching Gene devour her onion rings with obvious relish.

''You bet. I met this girl from Purchasing and—''

"No." Philip slapped his hands on the table.

"What?" Gene asked, jumping.

"Leave her alone."

"You don't even know who she is."

"It doesn't matter. Stay away from the help, Gene."

"Excuse me? The help?" His tone was teasing, but the look in his eyes was anything but.

"You know what I mean," Philip said softly, too softly.

Madalyn shivered and it had nothing to do with the wind.

Gene's smile contained more challenge than humor. "Are you trying to tell me who I can see?"

"I'm telling you to find someone besides an Ambercroft employee."

Gene cast a pointed look at Philip, then at Madalyn, then back to Philip. "Uh-huh."

"This is nothing like what I'm talking about," Philip said fiercely.

"Uh-huh," Gene said again as he stood. "Well, it's been fun, kids, but I'm supposed to meet Angela at the Runaway Mine Train in ten minutes. Gotta run."

He was gone before Philip could say another word. Madalyn was somewhat amazed to have been witness to this little family squabble, and watched in fascination as Philip threw his napkin down and sat back with a huff. Multimillion-dollar negotiations didn't make the man break a sweat, but a twelve-second conversation with his brother stole his appetite and obviously frustrated him.

"I don't know what I'm going to do with him," Philip muttered.

"Why do you have to do anything at all?" Madalyn asked.

He glanced up sharply. "I'm the head of the family, that's why."

She searched for the right diplomacy. "Philip, how old are you?"

"Almost forty," he answered with obvious question in his voice.

"And how old is Gene?"

"Thirty-three."

"And how staid and serious were you at thirty-three?"

"Very. I was already managing a huge portion of the company."

"Uh-huh." She nodded sagely. "And how much responsibility has Gene been given to this point? I know he has a *job*, but you haven't given him any *power*."

Philip's look was intimidating, but she didn't back down. She would be job hunting again anyway, and whether it was sooner or later really wasn't that big of a deal.

"And even more, you treat him like a child. He's an adult in case you hadn't noticed."

"I noticed," he said tersely. "Gene seems to be the one who hasn't made the connection."

She sighed. "Have you always been this controlling?"

"Excuse me?"

"Controlling," she repeated slowly. "Look, Philip,

it's easy for an outsider to see that you've always been the favored older son. Groomed to be the heir to the empire. While Gene may not even want to be you, he probably wants to be a real part of the family business, and you won't let go of the reins even the tiniest bit to give him a chance. But he has pride, just like you, and he won't ask for favors like Oliver asking for another bowl of gruel.''

''How do you—''

''I know more than you'd probably like. I did a lot of research into Ambercroft long before I started working here. I have my own little stock portfolio and you—I mean Ambercroft—has always fascinated me. The article in *Money Today* was one of the most comprehensive I've ever read on your family.''

Philip grimaced.

''I know, it wasn't very flattering, but you don't have to be a psychologist to see that Gene wants you to respect him.''

''He has a damned odd way of showing it.''

''Somehow I doubt cozy conversations were your family's strong suit.''

''That's for sure.'' He looked at her for a long moment. ''You're pretty gutsy, you know that?''

She felt her face blanch, but she didn't falter. ''Really? Why? Because I'm not afraid to tell the emperor he's not wearing any clothes?''

Philip barked a laugh. ''Pretty much.''

Madalyn toyed with her soda straw. ''Well, the short of it is that I like you, Philip. And I like Gene. And even though I might be risking my future employment, I couldn't just sit here and watch you and

Gene and not say anything. It was probably pretty stupid of me.''

"No, just gutsy. And it's one of the reasons I really like you, too. I'm not saying you're right, but I'll think about your points. About Gene, I mean.''

"I'm glad. Now, let's see how long the line is for that virtual reality thing.''

Philip watched Madalyn clean the table with her usual efficiency, and dutifully followed her out of the eatery. He wasn't the following type, but he also wasn't stupid. Even if he didn't like hearing what she'd said, it made sense. Obvious sense. So much sense he wondered why he hadn't seen it for himself.

The wind caught Madalyn's ponytail and blew her soft, silky hair across his face. The gentle slap took his mind off his brother and firmly placed it back on the woman who'd managed to turn his life upside down and didn't even know it.

Maybe Gene's interruption was fortuitous. He had once again let his mind wander down a path he shouldn't. Madalyn deserved to have someone in her life who was as open as she was. She had made it abundantly clear she wouldn't be involved with an employer, and that was good thinking. He couldn't promise anyone anything right now. Even though he might have an odd thought or two about marriage, he was too busy to actually pursue such a commitment. And as to children, he remembered well seeing more of his nanny than his parents, and if he couldn't do a better job with his own, then he wasn't going to have them at all.

So why couldn't he get the image of Madalyn—in

his arms and in his bed—out of his mind? Why couldn't he consider pursuing her without marriage in the scenario?

Mostly because he would never be like the jerk who had hurt her so badly. Or maybe it was because he knew, deep down, that Madalyn didn't pursue relationships lightly. Or maybe he was sick and tired of casual affairs.

And this coming from a man who had sworn he would never risk his heart again. He'd done it once, and it had nearly killed him. So what was it about Madalyn that made him even consider something long-term?

Forcing his racing thoughts into submission, he concentrated on the activities ahead. They spent the rest of the day enjoyably, and when he delivered Madalyn back home, he was firmly in control again.

As he drove away, he knew it had nothing to do with "class" or wealth or any other irrelevant trappings. He couldn't pursue Madalyn because she would need something from him he could not give— his whole heart. And she deserved the whole package deal. He just wasn't the one who could give it to her.

Chapter Seven

Madalyn was grateful that her little lecture at the amusement park hadn't affected their work relationship. Philip had been decidedly more reserved the next day as well as the following week, but no less polite. She chalked it up to another big deal he had in the hopper, and concentrated on doing her work. She was beginning to see a pattern in his nature and the closer he came to the closing of a deal, the more quiet and introspective his manner. That was logical, she supposed, especially with someone as contained as Philip.

The result was that she hadn't seen nearly as much of him as she had previously, and he was going to be out of town for the entire next week. Realizing Mrs. Montague would be back soon made it all the more sad. It was for the best, no doubt, but knowing she maybe had one work week left with Philip was distressing.

Battling the usual Friday traffic had been bad enough without worrying about the inevitable. She had a thousand things to accomplish before the evening's festivities, so she made herself stop thinking about the end of her term as Philip's secretary. She'd left a message for him yesterday reminding him of the gala, but she doubted he needed her prompting. She was just so happy for Mrs. Price that she hadn't been able to resist the urge to slip the note on the stack of files she'd left for him. She knew he'd be in either later that night, or was probably at the office right now. Either way, she'd done all she could to make sure he would be there. Mrs. Price had been beside herself when Madalyn had relayed Philip's RSVP. It was quite a coup for the committee.

By the time she had Erin bathed, herself showered, and was putting on her makeup, the sitter arrived and had Erin fully entertained. It was probably for the best as baby drool and sequins didn't tend to go together. Her dress was hardly a designer original, of which there would be an abundance tonight, but she was not ashamed of her gown. Off the rack might be anathema to the patrons she'd be rubbing elbows with, but her job wasn't to impress anyone. Her job was to help make Mrs. Price's evening a success.

With plenty of time to spare, Madalyn had packed her evening bag with her cell phone, pager, lipstick, driver's license, keys and money. All that was left was to kiss Erin good-night and head out.

As she'd suspected, she was too busy at the gala to worry about Philip's appearance. Much, anyway. As she ran here, checked that, called this person, she only looked at the door a few dozen times. Even after a healthy crowd had arrived, she still managed to keep the count under fifty. Or maybe that was when she lost count.

When the door opened and her radar told her to look one last time, she wished she hadn't. At the threshold stood Philip, breathtakingly handsome in a tuxedo complete with snowy white shirt and black bow tie.

And on his arm was the most breathtakingly beautiful woman Madalyn had never seen.

She was most certainly not dressed in a gown off the rack. Her ice-blue sheath decorated with sparkling beads had to have been custom-made to fit every solid inch of her tall, curvy figure so perfectly.

For the first time in as long as she could remember, Madalyn felt self-conscious. It wasn't anything Philip had done—he hadn't even spotted her yet. It was because of the sudden and stabbing realization that the woman on his arm, whoever she was, was the perfect mate for someone like Philip. All they'd done was enter the room and begin chatting, but Madalyn could see the woman was poised and elegant and...and so damned beautiful Madalyn wanted to run or cry or rip the woman's eyes out. Such feelings were completely abnormal for her, and her stomach spasmed in response.

"Dear, are you all right?"

Mrs. Price's voice and gentle hand helped Madalyn regain her composure.

"I'm fine, thank you. Did you see who just came in?" she asked as a distraction.

Eva Price's eyes grew round as she looked in the direction Madalyn pointed. "Oh my gosh. He came." Eva turned to Madalyn and grabbed her arm. "Thank you, thank you, my dear."

"I didn't do anything," Madalyn demurred.

"I'm sure you helped somehow," Eva argued. "You've been such a joy to Mr. Price and me."

"Well, the feeling is mutual. Why don't you go out and greet your newest mark—I mean contributor," she teased around the lump in her throat when she accidentally looked at the tall blonde again.

"I'm surprised to see him here with her, I have to say," Eva said thoughtfully.

"Her?" Madalyn asked, maybe a touch too casually.

"Ramona Stonehall."

"Of the Manhattan Stonehalls?" Madalyn asked, more distraught than ever. She'd learned quite a few of the movers and shakers as she'd worked with Mrs. Price, and had become familiar with the names of people so far outside her sphere as to make her feel like a chimney sweep by comparison.

"Yes. There was quite a flurry of rumors going around a year or so ago that Ramona was going to be the one to get Philip to the altar, but then they stopped seeing each other rather abruptly. No one knows why."

"They look like the perfect couple," she said, unable to stop a choke.

Eva looked at her sharply, and realization dawned in her eyes. "Oh, honey, don't tell me—"

"What?" Madalyn managed, clear-voiced. "I just

said they look like the perfect couple.'' She busied herself by running her finger down the checklist on her clipboard and marking Philip's name.

"Madalyn, honey—"

"I'm going to supervise the kitchen. We wouldn't want to run out of canapés."

She hurried away before she had to say anything more. Although she fully intended to see the chef, she stopped by the rest room first and sent up a small prayer of thanks that it was empty. She grabbed a paper towel and wet it, holding the coolness to her forehead as she sank onto the antique couch in the antechamber.

She tried to tell herself that it was silly to be so devastated, but more than anything, seeing Philip with Ramona Stonehall had driven the final nail into her heart. It wasn't that Ramona was wealthy.... Well, it wasn't simply because she was wealthy. It was more a three-dimensional example of the differences between Philip's world and hers. She hated admitting that wealth was part of it, but the reality was wealth did play a role. Madalyn was a small-town girl who'd never had more than a hundred dollars in the bank until a few years ago. Philip probably used hundred-dollar bills to tip waiters.

She might know a salad fork from a shrimp tine, but it was so much more than that. It was a comfort zone, an "inbred" ability to work in that world.

Determined not to hide, she straightened her spine and went back to the ballroom, and soon found Philip at her side.

"Good evening, Madalyn."

She nodded, back in control once again. "Philip. I saw you a moment ago at the door. Your date is lovely."

"Actually, I wasn't planning on bringing a date," he said in a tone that implied he wondered how it had happened. "Ramona called this morning to tell me she was in town, and I wasn't on guard when she asked me if I was free for the evening. But it's just as well. I'm sure Ramona will make her father send in a huge donation."

"That's—that's wonderful."

"Madalyn, what's the matter?"

"I'm just feeling a bit uncomfortable," she answered truthfully. Honesty was her best defense anyway. She had never been good at acting, even when it may have served her in the long run.

"Why?" He sounded genuinely confused.

Accepting glasses of punch from a waiter, they moved toward the edge of the dancers where the big-band era music had the floor filled with fox-trotters.

"Won't Ramona be looking for you?"

"Don't try to change the subject. Why are you feeling ill at ease?"

If he wanted her to spell it out, she would. "I'm a third wheel, all right?"

"Because you don't have a date? Why didn't you tell me earlier? I would have been glad to escort you."

"No, Philip, not because I don't have a date. Because I don't belong."

His deepening confusion was sweet.

"I don't know how to spell it out for you gently,

Philip. It was no coincidence that you didn't see the Junior League on my résumé. The only reason I'm here is for Eva.''

He took a sip of his cool, crisp punch. ''I'm rarely obtuse, but you have me stumped. Are you honestly saying you don't belong here because you aren't wealthy?''

She had to laugh. ''And just how many other secretaries do you see here? How many even from middle management?'' She waved her hand to encompass the ballroom.

He looked around almost despite himself. ''Okay, you've got me. I guess I just didn't picture you as class conscious.''

Her next laugh was soft, sad. ''I have no lack of confidence when I'm in my element. But this is not it.''

''You have nothing to prove, Madalyn. Not a woman in this room can hold a candle to you.''

''What a sweet thing to say! Even if it is a blatant lie.'' Her chuckle softened the censure.

''I beg your pardon,'' he countered, clearly affronted. ''You are beautiful, talented and charming. I could name half the women in this room whose beauty is thanks to skilled surgeons and private trainers, whose only talent is spending Daddy's or their hubby's money and who wouldn't know charm or tact if one came up and bit them.''

His vehement words stunned her. He really thought she was beautiful? He was so practiced and polished in banal chatter, she had immediately dismissed his compliment. Was it remotely possible he wasn't being merely polite?

No, she told herself fiercely. And she had to stop even considering such a thing. She caught herself and put a hand on his arm.

"Philip, your defense is positively delightful, but misplaced. I'm not comparing myself to any of the attendees here tonight. I'm proud of my life and my accomplishments, but that doesn't mean I'm not realistic."

She took her hand away and barely managed a delicate sip from her glass when what she wanted was to toss the whole thing back in the hopes the ice chips would cool her heated skin.

"I can't believe we're standing here talking about class differences," she said, shaking her head.

"I confess I wasn't expecting that train of conversation, either."

"Quite a jump from a simple hello, huh."

They both laughed, and she breathed a touch easier.

"Would you like to dance?" Philip asked as he took her glass and gave both to another passing waiter.

More than anything, she wanted to say yes, but some modicum of sanity prevailed and she shook her head. "Thank you, no—"

"Philip! There you are. Shame on you for making me track you down."

The soft, slightly Eastern accent broke their eye contact. Madalyn looked at Ramona Stonehall and somehow summoned a smile despite the stabbing jealousy in her gut when Ramona slipped her hand around the curve of Philip's arm.

"Won't you introduce me?" Ramona prompted pointedly.

"Ramona, I'd like you to meet Madalyn Wier. Madalyn, Ramona Stonehall."

Madalyn offered her hand first. "It's a pleasure."

Ramona's eyes sparkled and her smile seemed genuine.

"Are you related to Tony Wier, of Riverdale Publishing? In New York?"

"No, my family is all from Louisiana."

"Oh, well." Ramona laughed. "You never know. The world is such a small place...."

Madalyn nodded politely.

"So how do you know Philip?" Ramona asked, giving his arm a little bump.

"We're...friends," Philip interjected with only the slightest pause.

Madalyn had no interest in any such games, even if she did appreciate Philip's misguided attempt to avoid any embarrassment for her. Except she wasn't embarrassed about who she was...or what she was.

"Actually, I'm his secretary. For the time being anyway."

Ramona's expression froze before she recovered beautifully. "Oh, I see. I didn't know Ambercroft was a sponsor of this event."

She directed the comment to Philip, but Madalyn responded. "It isn't. Just a generous donor hopefully. I'll spare you the long story, except to say I'm a friend of the chairwoman. I'm really more staff than guest.''

"Well, even so, that dress is lovely and I'm delighted to meet you."

Madalyn didn't want to believe the genuine warmth in Ramona's eyes. She didn't want to like the heir to a fortune so vast Madalyn couldn't conceive it. She wanted Ramona to be haughty and condescending. She wanted to see a cool disdain come over Ramona's eyes now that she knew Madalyn was of the working class. It had happened enough times since she'd begun working with Eva. A few on the committee genuinely couldn't have cared less and Madalyn was at ease with them. She felt a familiar ease with Ramona, and Madalyn hated wishing she didn't. She wanted to believe she was above such pettiness, but obviously she wasn't.

In some tiny part of her brain, she wanted any woman in Philip's social sphere to be a snippy bitch so she, Madalyn, could bring that down-home sweetness into his life. She was disgusted with herself for even thinking it. Her "poor but happy" stereotype was no more accurate than "rich and mean." Philip didn't need saving. From her or by her.

One more latent fantasy ground to dust.

While lost in her thoughts, Philip took Ramona's cue and excused them to lead her onto the dance floor. It hurt too much to watch, so Madalyn decided it was the perfect time to go check the kitchen.

She'd have to save the gut-wrenching sobs for later, in the privacy of her own home.

* * *

"I missed you at the gala last weekend," Madalyn teased the younger Ambercroft hunk. "I know you got an invitation because Philip had me send you one."

She was surprised when Gene had come to the office again. With Philip out of town, she had hardly expected his brother to show up.

Having Philip gone the entire week had actually been a blessing. It had allowed her to wallow in her misery for a few days, and then she'd pulled herself together. Just this morning she'd found her laughter again. Maybe she was going to make it after all.

"I don't do monkey suits unless I have to. Like the command performance at my mother's big party next Saturday. Who was the lucky recipient of your largesse last week?"

"The benefit was for the Pediatric AIDS League. Isn't your mother's for the Council for the Arts?"

"Yes, and aren't you suitably impressed?"

Madalyn laughed when he rolled his eyes.

Gene pretended to be stunned by an idea. "Hey, why don't you save me the humiliation of going stag and be my date?" He leaned closer and gave her a terrific puppy-dog look.

"Because she's going with me," Philip said, coming off the elevator.

"I am?" she asked, moving her attention to her newly arrived boss.

She knew Gene's come-on for the malarkey it was. He had a bevy of women to choose from at any given moment. If he went stag anywhere, it was by his own choice.

"Yes, you are," Philip confirmed. "It's a command performance for me, as well, and I'd rather be there with someone who has something to talk about besides their newest tennis coach."

She wasn't sure how she was supposed to take that, as Ramona Stonehall had at least given the impression of intelligence. She chose to take it as a compliment.

"And why should you get her?" Gene asked in a tone that could only be described as aggrieved. "I asked first."

"Because she's my secretary. Besides, I've been out of town for a week and I don't have time to look for a date."

That was such blatant balderdash, Madalyn nearly choked on a laugh.

"That's ridiculous, Philip," she said without hesitation.

"Damn straight," Gene agreed.

Philip's face became closed and stern, the expression that said he'd made a decision and that was final. "Unless there is some reason you cannot join me?"

His tone fairly dared her to give him a lame excuse. She wasn't sure what was up with him, but she was sure she didn't want to challenge him at the moment.

"Um, no, that would be fine."

"Good. Gene," he said, pivoting his fierce look to his brother, "if you're here to see me, please come into my office."

Gene followed him in and Philip shut the door,

hoping his face didn't reveal how big a fool he felt like. He couldn't explain what had come over him when he'd stepped off the elevator and seen Gene flirting with Madalyn. He'd wanted to grab his little brother by the collar and give him the bum's rush.

Then to hear Gene ask her out on a date had been the topper. While he knew good and well that Gene was a heck of a guy under that irrepressible playboy façade, that didn't make Philip feel in the least better. The last thing Madalyn needed was to fall for a guy like Gene. A short fling was his style, and while the ladies Gene entertained never complained, Madalyn wasn't the fling type. He doubted Madalyn could resist if Gene put on his full-wattage charm, and it was up to him to protect her.

Besides, the devil on Philip's shoulder whispered into his ear, if Madalyn was even going to consider a fling, it had damn sure better be with him.

"What in the hell is wrong with you?" Gene demanded, breaking Philip's reverie.

"What do you mean?"

"That little he-man stunt out there. And playing dense doesn't suit you."

Philip straightened his jacket, pulling his cuffs down sharply. "No, I don't suppose it does. I'm not really sure what to say, except stay away from my secretary."

Gene gave him a sour look. "That old saw? Come on, Philip, give it a rest—"

Philip slapped his hand on the desk. "I mean it.

Madalyn is not some party girl looking for a wild weekend. Leave her alone.''

Gene's expression turned thoughtful and amused. "Boy, you've got it bad, don't you?"

"Don't be ridiculous.''

"I'm not. And I'm positively overjoyed to have ammunition of this caliber against you. You can hardly scold me when you've got the hots for your secretary.''

"I do not—''

"Don't deny it. I thought for a minute you were going to punch my lights out. You've never acted like a wet cat with any woman before. What else could it be?''

Philip decided he'd had enough of this particular conversation. "I'm sure you didn't come up here to discuss my love life,'' he said pointedly. "Do you need something?''

Thankfully Gene let the conversation be turned, and Philip listened to his brother's business proposition with only half a mind.

The other half was wondering what he was going to do with this case of the "hots'' he had for Madalyn....

After Gene left, Philip stepped out of his office to tell the object of his...thoughts...to go home. It was Friday, and close enough to five to call it a day. He knew she'd stay late since he'd just gotten back, but he wasn't about to ruin her weekend merely because he wouldn't see daylight until heaven only knew when.

He stopped when he saw a stricken look on her face. "Madalyn? What's wrong?"

"My aunt just called. My mother has fallen and broken her hip, and I've got to get home and see about her. My aunt is too frail to take care of her by herself and—"

Madalyn squeezed her eyes shut to stop the tears that threatened. She hadn't had to face her mother's aging in such a dramatic way before, and it had her more upset than she'd anticipated. She'd been fine on the phone with Aunt Liz, but as soon as she'd hung up, it had struck her what had happened.

It was so easy to pretend her mother wasn't getting fragile, that her bones weren't weakening, her eyesight failing... Madalyn just couldn't face being an orphan just yet, and Erin needed her granny. Mama was the only one either of them had.

She didn't realize she was crying until she felt Philip pull her into his arms. When her head touched his chest, it was as though a dam had burst and she could no more stop the flood than she could have stopped Niagara Falls. Hating herself for being weak, she sobbed against him.

"I just can't lose her," she whispered brokenly against the fabric of his jacket.

"Hey," he said soothingly, brushing her hair off her forehead with gentle fingers, "she's going to be fine. A broken hip isn't the end of the world."

Madalyn pulled away and composed herself. She found a tissue and blew her nose, and tried for a watery smile.

"You don't understand. They're talking hip replacement surgery. Medicare is only going to cover a fraction of that. Then the rehab—" She stopped herself short when she realized she was babbling. "I'm sorry. I didn't mean to go on like that."

She couldn't look at him as she straightened her desk. "I'm just about caught up, so if it's all right, I'm going to go ahead and leave. Erin and I have a long drive ahead of us."

"Why don't you let me fly you home. I can have the jet ready—"

"No. Thank you."

"But—"

"No. I...um...realize this really is the last straw. I have no idea if I can be back by Monday so—"

"Madalyn, if you haven't learned anything, haven't you figured out that your job is secure?"

"Well, no, actually. Missing one day for a sick child is hardly the same thing."

"Then let me make this clear. You are guaranteed to have a job here when you get back. Do not worry about that."

"Thank you." She sighed silently in relief. She was already imagining having to liquidate all her stocks and savings to take care of her mother. She had no qualms whatsoever about doing it, but it did make job security a harsh reality. At least she wouldn't have to job hunt at the same time. Not for the first time she wished her mother and aunt weren't so stubborn and would move closer.

"Now, about that plane—"

"Philip, no. Your offer is more than generous, but I can't let you."

"Why not?"

She sighed, aloud this time. "Do you offer the corporate jet to every employee who has a crisis?"

"No, but what does that—"

"I can't accept preferential treatment, Philip. It wouldn't be right. If Mother had had a heart attack, I'd probably jump on your offer, but a seven-hour drive is livable under the circumstances."

"That's nonsense—"

"Maybe to you, but not to me. Besides, if I flew, I'd have to rent a car and that would be a sheer waste of money."

"I'll rent you a car, dammit—"

"For the last time, no!" She hadn't realized she'd raised her voice until she saw his raised eyebrows.

"Please forgive me. I didn't mean to shout."

"That's all right, especially considering the stress you're feeling. I simply do not understand why you won't let me help you."

She had gathered her purse and jacket, and faced him again. "Because, Philip, I've been taking care of myself for a very long time. If I started accepting help from you now, what will I do when I'm down in the word processing pool and something else comes up? So thank you for your offer. It was kind. But I've made it on my own until now and I'll be making it on my own long after your life has returned to normal and I'm long forgotten."

She slung her purse over her shoulder and moved

to the elevator. "I left the numbers for my mother's house and the hospital on the desk in case you can't find something."

The doors slid open and she stepped in. She didn't say another word as the doors whispered shut.

"Stubborn woman," Philip muttered into the silence. He stared at the elevator for a long time.

Chapter Eight

The drive home was unremarkable, although Madalyn knew she was going to pay dearly for the long nap Erin had been lulled into by the road. It was almost three in the morning by the time she pulled into the driveway and lifted Erin from her car seat.

The porch light was on, but the window to Aunt Liz's room was dark. Madalyn hoped she was getting some sleep. Her mother and Aunt Liz were as close as any two sisters could be, but neither was in perfect health. She worried about both women, now more than ever.

She tried to be quiet, but Aunt Liz had never been a sound sleeper. She came into the guest room just as Madalyn was pulling a soft blanket over Erin in the crib.

"Lord, shay, you should'a waited until morning to drive all this way with that baby."

"I'm fine, Aunt Liz," she assured the older woman, giving her a warm buss on the cheek as she passed to go outside. "I'll be right back."

Two trips to the car later, she had all the bags and paraphernalia in the house and the door shut and locked.

"I made you some tea, shay. Then you need to get to bed."

"You're a sweetheart," she said, taking the cup Liz held out.

"Have you talked to your mama?"

"No, I called before I left Dallas, but she was asleep. I talked to the charge nurse while I was on the road, and she said Mama was doing well. Or as well as can be expected."

Sudden tears filled Liz's eyes. "I done tol' that old fool not to be going down those steps in her slippers. I said, 'You old fool, you gonna fall and break your fool neck.' But does she listen to me? Pshaw, like she ever listens to anyone. And what happens? You see what—"

"Aunt Liz," Madalyn interrupted gently, handing over a tissue from the ever-present box on the side-board. "It's all right. Mama's going to be fine."

"Would serve her right iffen it didn't. I get so mad at her—"

"And she gets just as mad at you. And you both love each other to death."

Liz sniffed. "Humph. As if that matter'd now to none."

Her façade broke and a tear slipped down her cheek. "I don't know what we gonna do, shay. Them doctors say she has to have surgery, and you know old people don't do good in surgery. And I don't know how we gonna pay for all this.''

Madalyn covered the blue-veined hands making a wreck out of the tissue. ''You will stop worrying right this minute. I have some money I've been saving for a rainy day.'' She tried for a bright smile. ''I'd say it's pouring, wouldn't you? So we're going to be fine.''

Liz answered her smile with a frown. ''Now you listen to me, shay. I'm just being a whining old woman. That money is for you and that baby. You got no husband to take care of you, and you need that money for yourself.''

Madalyn knew it was no use trying to convince Aunt Liz that she didn't need a husband any more than she'd been able to convince her mother, so she let it drop. Didn't anyone believe she could take care of herself?

''Well, we'll talk about this later. That angel you spoke of is going to be off schedule so I'd better grab some sleep while I can.'' Madalyn stood and moved around the table to give her aunt another big kiss on the forehead. ''You get some rest, too, and we'll go see Mama in the morning.''

''You are a good girl, shay. You always was.''

''Good night, Aunt Liz,'' she said fondly.

After rinsing out their cups and turning off the lights, Madalyn indulged in a long, hot shower before slipping on a nightgown and crawling between the clean, crisp sheets that smelled like home.

A good girl, huh? Madalyn punched her pillow.

She wasn't feeling like a good girl at the moment. She was feeling cranky and stressed and short-tempered. She was worried, afraid she was failing as a parent and desperately in love with a man who was hopelessly out of her reach. She didn't think she could take much more. Everyone needed her to be strong, and her shoulders were feeling the strain.

She punched the pillow the other way and refused to give in to the urge to dive into the pity pool. Whining never changed anything.

For all her stern lecture, her dreams weren't nearly as practical. Shining armor, white horses and Philip were the overwhelming themes.

Madalyn was surprised to find the room so bright when she awakened. She cast a bleary eye at the clock and sat bolt upright. Eight-fifteen!

Throwing the covers off, she leapt to the crib, her heart pounding. Something had to be wrong.

But the crib was empty.

Then she heard Erin's belly laugh, easing her fear before it could escalate into true panic.

Madalyn was thrusting her arms into her robe as she padded down the hall to find Aunt Liz on the living room floor with Erin, and every single toy Madalyn had brought strewn around them.

"Aunt Liz, are you crazy?" she scolded, coming into the room. "You're going to be the one with the broken hip, lolling on the floor like that."

Liz looked at Erin and shook her head. "I tol' you to be quiet, missy. I tol' you your mamma was gonna be cranky when she got up."

Erin blew a raspberry in response, grinning at her great-aunt.

Madalyn helped Liz to her feet and tried to keep her expression stern, but it was useless. She laughed and gave Liz a hug.

"And you call Mama stubborn," Madalyn said as she went over to the counter and poured herself a cup of coffee.

The living room blended into the kitchen in the tiny house she'd grown up in, but it somehow made the atmosphere seem cozy. It probably should have felt cramped, but Madalyn had never felt that way, not when the walls had been nearly bursting with all the love stuffed inside. Maybe that was what gave her the strength to keep going with a smile on her face. She could be bitter and angry, shaking her fist at the sky for life being unfair. But silly pipe dreams and all, her mother and father had made her childhood memorable.

She shook her head and took a sip of chicory coffee. "You should have gotten me up, Aunt Liz. We could be at the hospital already."

"I done talked to the nurse and she said they was doing X rays and some physical therapy this mornin' so there was no sense in comin' in until ten o'clock or so. She won't even be in her room."

Madalyn was anxious to see her mother, but Aunt Liz was right. It made no sense to sit in an empty room. "Thanks for letting me sleep in, then. It's been years since I've had that luxury."

"We're worried about you, shay. Your mama and me. You bein' alone and all."

"I've told you both a thousand times that I'm just fine. I can take care of Erin and myself."

"But—"

A knock interrupted their oft-repeated argument. Madalyn was grateful.

Liz squealed a moment later, making Madalyn slosh hot coffee on her hand as she slammed her cup down to hurry to the front door.

"Shay! Come he'ya and look at this."

This was a huge bouquet of pale pink roses being delivered. Liz signed the log book while Madalyn carried the vase inside.

"Who they from?" Liz asked, as excited as a child at Christmas.

Madalyn was fairly sure she knew, but the card confirmed it.

"'Madalyn, forgive me for stepping on your pride,'" she read aloud. "'I hope your mother is well soon. Philip.'"

"Oooh, shay, you didn't tell me you had a beau!"

"I don't."

"Why, sure you do. A man don't send flowers like that unless he's serious."

"He's my boss, not my beau. He's just being nice."

"...twenty-three, twenty-four. Mmm-hmm. And how many bosses send twenty-four roses to someone they just bein' nice to, I ask you?"

"Aunt Liz, this man could send two dozen roses to every woman he knows and it wouldn't put a dent in his pin money. There is nothing more to this than a nice gesture."

"Mmm-hmm."

Madalyn threw up her hands and conceded. "If you don't mind watching the munchkin, I'm going to go take a shower."

Even lollygagging, they arrived at the hospital before Carolina was back from a consultation with the physical therapist. The lag time gave Madalyn a chance to talk to her mother's doctor, and she also spoke with a geriatric orthopedic specialist. She had a better handle on what to expect, and that alone was a great relief.

But it wasn't until she actually saw her mother that Madalyn felt at peace. Carolina looked wonderful, all things considered. And despite the faint pain lines on her face, Carolina crowed with delight when she saw Erin.

"The doctor says you're not taking much pain medication, Mama. Are you sure you're not hurting too much?"

"I'm fine, shay. I don't like that woozy feelin' in my head. I take enough to be okay, don't you worry."

For someone who believed in fairy tales, her mother could be impossibly practical and pigheaded sometimes.

Her daddy had always said she was just like her mother, which Madalyn still denied.

Liz was about to faint from wanting to tell Carolina about the flowers. Madalyn groaned and put her head in her hands as the two women discussed the "obvious" portent of the roses. When a huge spring bouquet was delivered to Carolina a short while later, the two were beside themselves. Any man who sent flowers to a girl's mother *had* to be serious.

Madalyn wanted to kill Philip.

"Mama, neither your flowers nor mine have any deeper meaning than kindness. Philip can be very generous, and he—"

"He's sweet on you, shay. Oh, this is just wonderful!"

"He is not sweet on me," Madalyn said through gritted teeth.

"I'm tellin' you—"

"And I'm telling *you*, just as I told Aunt Liz, that Philip is my boss. Only my boss. He just happens to be a nice man."

"A very rich nice man," Carolina said in an aside to Liz.

That was the last straw for Madalyn. "Just stop it, will you please! Just when I get a handle on those stupid fairy tales you stuffed into my head, something happens to rock my equilibrium. I'm telling you for the last time that there is no happily-ever-after."

Feeling awful, she grabbed Erin and stormed out. She didn't stop walking until she found the pediatric wing and a nearly empty playroom. A nurse said it was okay to take Erin inside, and Madalyn curled into a ball in a chair as Erin gleefully attacked a blow-up clown bobbing in the center of the room.

Raking her hair out of her face, Madalyn tried for all she was worth to get her blood pressure down. She hadn't wanted to hurt either her mother or her aunt, but she had to make them listen. It made her mad, and at the same time made her laugh, that they got so excited and happy about even the prospect that there was a man in her life. As if that was the be-all and end-all of existence. She knew they meant well, that they were a product of not only their generation, but their Southern culture, and for them, being married was a crowning achievement. But they had to give up this crazy fantasy about her life. She doubted she'd ever get married, and she sure as heck wasn't going to be marrying her boss.

God forbid if they found out how madly in love she was with Philip....

Her heart hurt and her nerves were raw. She simply couldn't take it if they kept it up.

When Erin started to get cranky, Madalyn sought out one of the rockers placed around the room, and let the soothing rhythm and sweet baby sighs take the rest of the edge away.

By the time she returned to the room, she was collected and ready to give a heartfelt apology.

"Mama," Madalyn said quietly over Erin's sleeping head, "please forgive me. I was harsh and I was wrong—"

"Now you listen he'ya, shay. You got nothing to apologize for. We're just two old matchmaking biddies and we was wrong. We're the ones who's sorry."

"Oh, Mama," she said, taking her mother's hand into hers, "I wish you could be right. I wish there were happy endings to every story. There just aren't."

Carolina looked at the flowers on her windowsill and just smiled.

Philip decided he was losing his mind. Mrs. Montague was nigh unto the perfect secretary, and he'd hidden his panic when she'd asked to take a long stretch of well-earned vacation time. Then he'd found Madalyn, and decided she was proof that lightning could strike twice.

Now Madalyn was gone, and he wondered if he could find his own hind end with both hands. Worse, she was all he could think of. Which was one reason he wasn't getting any work done.

She was coming back today, thank heaven. How he'd made it to Wednesday was nothing short of a miracle.

He wondered if his excuses to call had sounded as lame to her as they had to his own ears, but he'd needed to hear her voice. Not for any romantic reason, of course. It was just this silly mild panic. Besides, he'd wanted to make sure her mother was all right.

When the elevator bell chimed, his pulse jumped at least thirty points. He worked to school his features into a calm mask before he turned around.

"Welcome back," he said, deliberately pretending to scan a file before snapping it shut.

"I can see you were too busy to miss me much," she noted with a nod toward her desk, adding a smile.

"On the contrary," he objected. "I missed you terribly. You know I hate those little tape things, but I've had to make do."

She laughed and shrugged out of her jacket. She all but rolled up her sleeves, and he could tell she was ready to jump right in.

"How is your mother doing?"

"She's going to be fine. And she loved her flowers,

by the way. My roses were beautiful, too. Thank you.''

"You're welcome. What about surgery?''

"They've decided against it, for now. I have her set up with the best physical therapist in the area, and although she'll be on a walker for a long time, eventually they expect her to be fully mobile again.''

The delightful flush that suffused her face when she was embarrassed was back.

"Now that you have more information than you wanted, let me summarize by saying she's doing great.''

It was one of those things that he hadn't even realized he'd missed until he'd seen it again. Her blushes were so much a part of her, like her spontaneity. For all her professionalism, for all that life had thrown a real knuckle ball in her direction, she retained an inner joy that leaked out even when she didn't want it to.

"I'm glad to hear that, Madalyn. I know you were beside yourself with worry.''

She blushed again. "Um, about that. I can't apologize enough—''

"Not another word. It's forgotten. Now, let's see if I can earn my reputation as a slave driver and get caught up.''

She chuckled, obviously undaunted by his threat.

Probably because she'd amazed him with her ability to keep up with him.

He retreated to his office, only to stop and look around the doorjamb at her. "Don't forget about Saturday.''

"Saturday?"

"I'll pick you up at six for my mother's gala."

"Oh, yes. That would be fine."

Philip shut his door and wondered why he was suddenly anxious for the work week to be over.

Chapter Nine

Saturday turned out to be another glorious Texas spring day with brilliant blue skies and temperatures in the low seventies. After a morning spent chasing Erin through fields of bluebonnets and Indian paintbrush to get an Easter picture, Madalyn was energized. She supposed she should have been exhausted, but even Erin's limitless energy hadn't taken away the building excitement of the evening ahead. Madalyn kept trying to put her errant thoughts in order, tried to convince herself this was no big deal, but she wasn't succeeding.

They returned home and she lay down herself after she put Erin in her crib, something Madalyn never did. The few precious hours Erin slept were reserved for chores that couldn't be done with a toddler underfoot, or even something as decadent as indulging in a cup of coffee and a book by her favorite author.

When the doorbell rang, she groaned and hauled herself off the couch, muttering that was what she got for thinking she could get a nap.

Her sleepy brain instantly cleared of fog when the messenger handed her a box tied with an elegant satin bow. Bemused, she signed her name and took the intriguing package inside. She settled on the couch and found a small envelope bearing the understated but elegant embossing of one of the most exclusive boutiques in town. She pulled out the note card and instantly recognized Philip's handwriting. The card read, "Don't argue. Just enjoy."

Slipping off the bow, she opened the box.

And gasped.

Nestled in tissue paper was a beaded jacket in peach silk. Two-millimeter pearls and tiny crystal bugle beads covered the long-sleeved, short-waisted vision. Under the jacket was a sleeveless, A-line dress in the same peach silk, but it was covered with a layer of sheer organza. She stood and held the dress against her, twirling in a circle. The full skirt swirled around her and floated to a graceful stop.

She'd never seen such a beautiful dress in her life. And she'd never dreamed of owning one, either.

Hurrying to her room, she stripped off her sweats and pulled on the dress. Her hair got in the way, and with a frustrated twist, she pinned it back, wishing she hadn't lost her glazed chopsticks in Alabama. They were her favorite easy-and-elegant accessory, and they were the perfect color. Instead she used pearl-studded combs.

The dress fit as though custom-made for her. The

bodice was snug without being tight. The skirt belled from the waist to rest just below her ankles. Digging in her closet, she found the ivory satin pumps she'd bought just two weeks before and stepped into them. Lastly, she held her breath as she slipped on the bolero jacket. She couldn't believe it. Even without makeup, it was as though her fairy godmother had waved a magic wand and replaced Madalyn Wier, harried single mom, with Madalyn Wier, temporary princess.

As she looked in the mirror, the smile slipped from her face. Could she play Cinderella? Could she have just one ball with her prince and survive a return to the scullery? She knew that for her there would be no glass slipper.

Taking a deep breath, she decided that yes, she could have this one night. She accepted that she was facing a lifetime of paycheck-to-paycheck living, just as her parents had. She was entitled to grab a moment such as this, for the memories if nothing else. Her mother had sung her the siren song for so long, she was almost helpless to resist the lure of one night in the fantasy.

Almost, but not quite.

If she was going to do this, she was going to do it with her eyes wide open. No crying foul if her heart got broken. But then again, how could it be any more broken than it was already? She'd already accepted that Philip wasn't hers, could never be. So what harm was there in taking this one night and enjoying it to the fullest?

Without answering herself, she took off the gown

and laid it carefully on her bed. A glance at the clock said she had four hours. If she hurried, she could get in a decadent bubble bath before Erin awoke. The sitter was coming at five, which left her plenty of time to get ready before Philip arrived at six. She assumed they were going to dinner since the gala didn't start until eight. He hadn't said, but that was the only logical explanation.

But as with the best-laid plans, it was five before she knew it, and she was blow-drying her hair when the sitter finally came over so Madalyn could finish dressing without risking spaghetti sauce fingers on her exquisite dress.

When Philip arrived, she was a bundle of nerves. She'd redone her hair at least seven times before she was satisfied with the lay of the twist and the wispy spirals she'd left at her ears.

She'd scrubbed her makeup off and started over twice.

She'd even wondered several times, before getting a grip, if she could make it to the shoe store and back.

Then he walked into her home, in that incredibly fitting tuxedo, his hair styled back, his cologne crisp and faintly spicy. Her knees had gone all weak on her and she'd been glad she was standing behind the rocker, using a game of peek-a-boo with Erin as an excuse to keep her sweet child occupied without touching. Now she clutched the varnished slats as though her life depended on it. At the least, her dignity did.

"Good evening."

Lord above, even his voice was beautiful. She

knew that, having listened to it every day for the last month. But tonight was different. It sounded deeper, huskier. She knew it was her imagination, but even so, it slid over her nerves as smoothly as the dress had slid over her hips.

"You look wonderful," she breathed.

And immediately blushed.

His chuckle was deep, too. "That's supposed to be my line."

"Oh, sorry."

The moment was broken by Erin. Toddling as fast as her little legs could carry her, she took a toy over and offered it up to Philip.

Madalyn interpreted for him. "She wants you to take it."

"Why?"

"So you can give it back to her."

"Oh." He nodded sagely. "That makes perfect sense."

Hitching his pants at his knees, he squatted down and took the toy. Madalyn was impressed. He didn't flinch at the slightly slobbery texture.

"Thank you," he said gravely.

As she'd predicted, Erin had grinned and taken the toy right back. Then she did something that utterly amazed Madalyn. She held out her arms in the universal "pick me up" gesture.

He looked at Madalyn, confused.

"She wants you to pick her up."

"Really?"

"Really. And I have to tell you that while Erin is very social, she doesn't do this with everyone."

With utter care, Philip picked Erin up and stood. "I'm suitably humbled."

Erin bubbled happily and grabbed at the rose in his lapel.

Madalyn rushed over to intercede, grabbing a towel as she flew by. The rose was saved, and Madalyn wiped Erin's face before any stains could get on Philip's tuxedo. Despite the touching moment, she called the baby-sitter over and had her take Erin off to play. There was no sense in tempting the Fates too much.

With goodbyes to Erin and the sitter, Philip escorted Madalyn out to the limousine, complete with chauffeur waiting by the passenger door. And from that moment on, the evening became surreal.

From champagne in the limousine to dinner at a restaurant so exclusive they never advertised—which explained why Madalyn had never heard of it—to coffee and dessert at a bistro downtown, she felt transported to another world. She heard music from Rachmaninoff in the limo, a string quartet at the restaurant, and jazz at the bistro. If the limo had sprouted spoked wheels and if a tail had appeared under the driver's jacket, she wouldn't have been surprised. It merely would have proven her suspicion that this was all a magical dream.

"Did you catch the speech by the Secretary General of the United Nations on C-Span?"

She looked at Philip and burst out laughing. She knew he was pretending to be pompous to get a rise out of her, but it amused her more than he bargained for.

"Are you kidding? I don't even know who the man is. And I wouldn't get to watch C-Span unless Barney was making a guest appearance."

"Barney?"

"The purple dinosaur?"

"Oh, yes. He's still around?"

"Let's just say he's a classic."

"I wonder why people say he's insipid, then."

"You know, I hear that a lot, but it boggles me as to why people think teaching children they're loved, promoting values like honesty, and behavior like when to use their quiet voice, is so bad."

Madalyn realized he was fighting a grin and she bristled. "Oh, you!" she groused, resisting the urge to throw her napkin at him. "I sure bit on that one, didn't I?"

"To be honest, I never imagined my opening gambit would lead to a discussion about purple dinosaurs. I figured we'd get into a rousing political debate, but I'm not complaining. Talking with you is always fascinating. You see things so differently than I do."

"Big surprise. I'm sure it has a touch to do with the fact that I'm female and a mother." She paused and let the waiter fill her cup. "It tends to change your focus a bit."

Philip nodded for the check, then took a sip from his own refreshed cup. "I see that now, as I never have before. You've been good for me, Madalyn."

She hid her inability to come up with a suitable response behind a smile and sip.

"You threw me with that C-Span thing. I thought

you weren't supposed to talk about politics, religion or money in a social setting."

"Just call me a rebel."

He was so droll she nearly choked on her coffee.

"Besides, our rousing debates have been great. You see things from such a different perspective. It intrigues me."

She felt a stab near the region of her heart. She put her cup down slowly and met his eyes.

"You mean from a *common* perspective?"

He looked so stunned, she knew she had jumped to the wrong conclusion.

"No," he denied softly, vehemently. "From a *unique* perspective."

"Let me give you a little clue, Philip. There are millions of single parents in America today. That hardly makes me unique."

"That may be true, but I was thinking more about the fact that you aren't afraid of me, Madalyn. You neither think me some kind of god—an image which I do not covet despite articles to the contrary—nor do you fear me. You tell me straight what you're thinking, and you argue with me when you think I'm wrong about something."

Her shame at leaping to conclusions was only compounded by his sincerity.

"I can't tell you how much I wish I could take that comment back."

It was fortuitous that the check arrived and moments later they were on their way to the gala. The awkward moment was forgotten, and Philip soon had her in fits of laughter with his imitations of some of the people who would be at the event. Knowing a number of those people from her work with Eva, the dead-on accuracy of his impersonations only made her laugh harder.

Philip had timed them to arrive fashionably late. A crowd had already assembled, judging from the number of limousines parked along the long road leading to his ancestral home. As was his privilege, he had the driver take them around back to avoid the congestion.

She knew a bit about the Ambercroft mansion from her reading, but it hadn't done justice to the incredible building before her. She knew even less about architecture, but she was fairly sure the style was antebellum. Rumor had it that the mansion had been built on a legacy from Philip's great-grandfather's still. It was said that Philip's grandfather had made a fortune running the family brew during Prohibition. Then he had turned *respectable*, and the rest was history.

She didn't even try to estimate the square footage, since she confessed to being spatially challenged, but by craning her head back, she could follow generations of ivy climbing the red brick exterior all the way to the roof line three stories overhead.

He asked her preference, and instead of going through the house to the ballroom, she chose walking around to the front and up the steps to the massive, columned porch. The view from the front was spectacular, and her horticulturist's heart was awed by the intricate landscaping still visible in the early twilight. She could only imagine the glory of the flowers in full bloom under bright sunlight.

She wasn't given long to enjoy the view as the crowd pulled them in among the throng. Between introductions she was able to glance around the foyer—which alone seemed bigger than her little tract home. The wood floor gleamed with innumerable layers of bright, clear wax. The magnificent staircase claiming the center of attention was something out of *Gone With The Wind.*

The ballroom was a few paces back on the left side, yet another room out of some kind of fantasy. Philip led her through more introductions before they finally found his mother.

Mrs. Olga Ambercroft's smile slipped ever so slightly when she heard Madalyn's name, but her tone was painfully polite when she asked if she could speak to Philip for a moment. Not even hearing Mrs. Ambercroft whispering vehemently to Philip and catching *secretary, date* and *missed opportunities* could dampen Madalyn's spirits.

When he rejoined her, she noticed his jaw was tight.

"Guess you got scolded, huh," she said, trying to lighten the moment.

Philip's eyes lost their sternness and a twinkle returned. "Something like that. My mother is a tad concerned I didn't bring a date with more...um...donor potential."

"Hey, I've got a twenty tucked into the lining of my purse," she retorted with a cheeky grin. "Should I turn it in now?"

Philip threw back his head and laughed, earning them more than one curious glance. Her saving grace in all this was her refusal to pretend she was something that she wasn't. Her lack of embarrassment over her circumstances freed Philip to join her in the humor of the situation.

"Shall I take you on the nickel tour?" he asked. "Or would you like to dance."

"Hmm, tough choice, but I think I'd like the tour, if you don't mind."

"Not a bit. This way."

When he put his hand on her elbow as he escorted her up the grand staircase, Madalyn shivered. Any time he touched her, she shivered. It was an automatic response to the hormones that raged through her when his skin was against hers. Even the jacket between his fingers and her arm was no protection. In fact, the sensual fabric only made it worse.

"Are you cold?" he asked, ever solicitous.

She felt more that she had a raging fever, but that would hardly be the appropriate response. "I'm fine. Just caught a draft, I think."

When they paused on the landing, she glanced at him from the corner of her eye and smiled. "I do hope the tour includes a peek at your nursery. Undisturbed by time, I'm sure, with little soldiers waiting frozen for the next generation of future world leaders to come play."

He took her teasing with his usual good grace. "Sorry, but no such sentimentality. My nursery is now a study, but I'll be glad to show it to you."

He opened the door and flipped the light switch, then stood back for her to enter.

"I have a confession to make," she said, glancing

around a room that was yet another testament to priceless antiques.

"Another confession? I'm agog with anticipation."

She shook her head and bit her lip to keep from grinning. "If you're going to be sarcastic, then I'm not saying another word."

He captured her arms as she started to move away. "Tell me."

She knew she couldn't maintain coy for long, so she relented. "When I first met you, I *was* one of those silly people you spoke of who thought you were a god. I'd read about you, about your family, and you weren't really human. Then, as I worked for you, I came to see you differently."

"Is that good or bad?"

"Definitely good." She stepped away and trailed her hand along the back of one of the requisite wing-backed chairs paired in front of the fireplace. She set her beaded bag on the arm of the chair with overt care. It gave her an excuse not to look at him while she continued.

"I just wanted you to know that this experience has been wonderful for me, and I'm grateful you gave me this chance. I know Mrs. Montague is going to be back soon, and I wanted to get that off my chest in case I didn't get another opportunity."

Philip followed her to where she stood looking at his father's portrait.

"Madalyn, just because—"

"You look like him, you know."

"So I've been told. Listen—"

"Gene looks more like your mother, but you both have strong Ambercroft genes."

"Madalyn—"

"Philip, don't." She placed her fingertips briefly against his lips. "Don't say we'll see each other. You'll be busy getting back into your normal routine, and I'll become secretary to one of your middle managers somewhere. If I'm lucky, I'll catch a glimpse of you at Six Flags next year."

"Madalyn," he said sternly, grabbing her fingers and kissing them, then pulling her close, "I'd like you to shut up now."

"Okay," she whispered, her eyes drifting shut as his mouth descended on her.

She'd been so hoping he'd kiss her. No goodbye was complete without one really good kiss.

And she was gloriously not disappointed.

He pulled her even closer, wrapping his arms around her and melding her to him. Twining her arms around his neck, she sighed and relaxed into his embrace.

His lips teased her, his hands roamed her, and none of it was enough. The teasing became demanding, and it was still not enough.

Demand became flame, burning her as she'd never felt before. She didn't even know she'd shed her jacket until she felt his hands on her arms, her shoulders, her back where her dress dipped low below her shoulder blades. His touch felt like liquid fire on her skin. Hot. Magical.

Her hands slipped inside his jacket, clutching his chest through his starched shirt. His muscles bunched under her fingertips, as though her touch burned him, too.

Her breathing was as ragged as his, her moans as unsatisfied.

"Yes," she whispered against his throat when she felt her zipper being pulled down.

"Yes," he repeated in hoarse agony as he bared one shoulder, covering the creamy white skin with his kisses.

"Ah-hem." The cough came from across the room.

Philip reacted as though stung. She yelped in stunned surprise when he thrust her from him, only to pull her behind him protectively. She glanced around him to see Gene sitting on the arm of a chair, one arm casually draped over the back, one leg swinging.

"What in the hell are you doing?" Philip demanded.

"Waiting for you two to come up for air. The way things were progressing, I decided that wasn't very likely."

Madalyn was grateful for the shield of Philip's body as she slipped her dress back in place, reaching behind her to pull the zipper up. Retrieving her jacket and putting it on saved her the humiliation of looking at either Philip or his brother.

"I'm going to find the ladies' room," she muttered, using the first excuse she could concoct to get away. She bolted for the door, desperate to escape, barely remembering to grab her purse on the way out.

When the door to the study shut behind her, a near-deafening silence fell between the brothers.

"What the hell am *I* doing?" Gene repeated Philip's demand. "Shouldn't the question be what the hell are *you* doing?"

"I do not have to explain my actions to you."

"That's rich, Philip. All right, I'll go first. I came in here for a cigar and a brandy. I didn't know a show came with it."

Gene's pointed glance had Philip buttoning his shirt and straightening his jacket.

"Just what are your intentions toward Madalyn?"

"My intentions?" Philip barked a laugh. "Who are you, her father?"

"No, but then, who are you?" Gene tapped his chin as though thinking. "Oh yes, I remember. You're her boss."

Philip looked away guiltily. "Touché."

Gene sighed. "I'm not here to spar with you, Philip. And blushing bronze isn't your color."

It took Philip a second to follow the segue. Then a blush of his own colored his cheeks as he reached into his back pocket for a handkerchief. He had enough grace to look at Gene with a questioning eyebrow raised after he'd wiped his mouth and chin. Gene pointed to a spot on his own jaw, and Philip got the last of the lipstick off.

"Listen, Philip, I—"

"Don't say anything. It's all right." He combed his fingers though his hair and took a deep breath. "It was probably for the best."

"Yeah, but being honorable sucks sometimes."

Philip smiled a bit sadly. "Mother hates it when you say *sucks.*"

"I know. It's so low-class. Don't you just love it?"

Shaking his head despairingly, he stood still when Gene walked over and straightened his bow tie.

Philip led the way out of the study, then stopped to offer his brother his hand. "You're right, though. It does suck."

Madalyn knew she couldn't stay in the bathroom all night, but the thought was tempting. Thank goodness she'd brought enough cosmetics to repair her face at least. Surely no one could tell just by looking that she'd been about to strip down in the home of *the* matron of Texas high society. And with said matron's golden son, no less.

Maybe the clock would strike midnight soon and she'd turn into a pumpkin. No, wait. That was the coach.... At the moment she'd take any transformation—rat, bat...whatever would get her away without having to face Philip again.

Gathering her courage, she finally left the lavatory and checked her hair at the mirror in the small anteroom one last time. Then the door opened, making her jump.

"There you are, my dear," Eva Price said, putting a hand on her arm. "Is something wrong? We've been looking for you."

"No, nothing's wrong," she lied behind a too-bright smile. "I'll go join Mr. Price."

"Wait—"

But she didn't. She couldn't endure a private interrogation. Eva was too much a mother hen to be put off and Madalyn couldn't face explanations just yet.

Besides, banal conversation was just what she needed to get through the rest of this evening. No real thought required.

Mr. Price gave her a fatherly kiss on the cheek when she found him. He saw she received a glass of champagne punch as they stood on the perimeter of the ballroom while the orchestra played and a host of dancers paid tribute to its talent.

"Did Eva find you, my dear?"

"Yes, we passed each other in the powder room."

He cleared his throat and lowered his voice. "Then she told you?"

"Told me? No, she didn't say anything."

He glanced around and inched closer. "We were hoping our son-in-law was going to be able to buy the business, but his capital venture fell through. It looks as though we'll be forced into receivership soon."

"Oh, I'm so sorry."

Mr. Price gave her a game smile and shrugged. "We'll be fine. I just wanted to be sure you sold that stock like I told you to."

"Yes, I did as you asked."

"Good." He rubbed his hands together and made a show of picking an hors d'oeuvre from a passing waiter's tray. "You really should try these," he said in a normal voice.

She was glad for the diversion, although she couldn't have swallowed if her life depended on it. She simply loved the Prices. They were dear people and she hated to see this happening to them. She struggled for a smile to maintain Mr. Price's jovial cover.

When Eva rejoined them, Madalyn excused herself. As she'd stood with Mr. Price, a plan that had been forming for some time jelled. Even though it would be difficult to face Philip, she was going to help the Prices...or at least try.

Chapter Ten

Madalyn went in search of Philip, her nerves a wreck, but determined to accomplish her mission. Her attention was so focused, she was startled when someone caught her arm and stopped her rather abruptly.

"Well, well, well. I must say I'm proud of you, Madalyn. You set your sights even higher than I did."

Her stomach immediately soured. "Eddie. How...nice to see you."

"So what's your angle? Are you trying to convince him he's the father of your little brat?"

Madalyn's blood turned to ice, and pure rage swept through her. Then she remembered the kind of man she was talking to, and wondered for the thousandth time how she'd ever thought she'd been in love with him. Of course, as he was being crude, it was easy to forget how suave and charming he could be when he wanted to be.

He wasn't worth her anger. He wasn't worth the expenditure of any emotion. Not for a man who was so shallow he'd deny himself the joy of a child like Erin. Of course, now that she knew him for what he was, she was secretly glad he had no part in Erin's life.

What she hated was the instant of doubt he planted in her mind, about her motives, about why she was there. It took a concerted effort, an effort she had to struggle not to resent, to check within herself and conclude she had no hidden agendas. She was harboring no secret hope that Philip would prostrate himself before her and beg her to marry him. She wasn't planning on somehow infiltrating the lives of the rich and famous. She was here as the date of her boss, yes, but it was for a good cause and merely a pleasant evening.

All her thoughts had taken a few seconds, and she returned her attention to Eddie with a small smile.

"What a...pleasure...to see you again, Eddie. If you'll excuse me?"

She didn't wait for a reply. She had no intention of spending one additional second in his company. And besides, she had just wasted several precious minutes that she could have spent with Philip. Minutes she hoped she could recapture and engage his help for the Prices.

By the time she found Philip talking to a group of older men by the bar, her equilibrium had returned. She had dismissed Eddie as the useless waste of oxygen he was and refused to give him any more thought.

Amazed at her own boldness, she stepped next to Philip and effectively interrupted the conversation.

"Excuse me, gentlemen, but could I steal Philip for a moment?"

Good breeding and the rules of etiquette prevented the gentlemen from objecting. Philip bowed his way out and strolled away with her.

"Could I speak with you? In private?"

Looking marginally nonplussed, he recovered instantly. "Of course. Let's go to the library. No one should bother us there."

She had no idea where the library was, of course, but she nodded and let him lead.

The library was done in more obscenely expensive antiques, all tastefully arranged and immaculately kept. She moved to the far wall and would have bet her life the Renoir before her was an original.

"Madalyn?"

She needed the prompting, but it still made her blush. "I need to discuss something of a rather delicate nature with you."

"Go on."

"You know how much I care for the Prices, and…" She pressed her fingertips to her forehead and took a deep breath. With one last battle with her conscience, she continued, although her agitated pacing took her around the room and back by the double door she'd just entered.

"You see, their business, their pride and joy, is going to be forced into receivership. Did you know that?"

Philip had his fingers on the pulse of the business

community, so she would have been surprised if he *hadn't* known, unless Price Manufacturing was too small to garner his notice.

"I've…heard rumors."

"What I'm about to ask is totally my idea, so if you say no, please don't tell the Prices. They'd be mortified to ask anyone for help."

"I suspect you're going to ask me to intervene on their behalf, possibly buy the company or extend a loan?"

"Well, yes," she said, feeling that awful desire for the floor to open up and swallow her. Having him all the way across the room was only marginally helpful. "They aren't too small, are they?"

"Madalyn, before we go any farther, I need to tell you something. I've had my eye—"

The doors burst open, one door nearly catching Madalyn full in the face as Philip's mother swept into the room.

"Philip! I've been looking everywhere for you. Paul Leffler overheard Martin Price talking to some girl—"

"Mother—"

"Price is going into receivership! Isn't that wonderful?"

The look on his face finally made Olga Ambercroft stop.

"Mother, I'd like to reintroduce you to Madalyn Wier." He waved toward the back of the room. "The woman Martin was talking to."

Madalyn was frozen. She couldn't speak. She could hardly breathe.

Olga misunderstood.

"Philip! How clever to have your secretary spy things out."

Madalyn noted, in some distant portion of her brain, that Philip's face had grown cold.

"She's not a spy, Mother. She is a former employee of the Prices and remains very close to them."

Olga finally made the connection. With no hint of embarrassment, she said, "Well, then. Forgive me for interrupting."

She swept out of the room with all the gale force she'd come in with. The room was left with the deadly calm after a storm had passed. Or perhaps just before one.

"You used me," she whispered past her stricken throat. "All this time, you were using me."

"Madalyn, no—"

She recoiled when he took a step toward her.

"Please listen to me. I didn't use you."

"So you weren't about to say you have had your eye on Price Manufacturing?"

He winced. "Yes, but I never once pumped you for information."

Her laugh was devoid of humor. "Why would you have, when I was practically spilling my guts to you?"

"You never did that, Madalyn. You were always careful what you said about the Prices."

"And like you haven't made a billion dollars by knowing how to read between the lines."

"I know I should have told you sooner. I was going to—"

"When? After I heard about it on *The Stock Market Today* on C-Span?"

"I thought you didn't watch C-Span."

She glared at him for his lame attempt at humor. With as much dignity as she could muster, she picked up her purse and pulled the door open.

"Goodbye, Philip."

She ignored his footsteps behind her and hurried through the house, using the milling guests to separate her from Philip. When she risked a glance, she saw him trying to extricate himself from several men who had stopped him to try to draw him back into their conversation.

She didn't look back again.

It took several frustrating minutes to get to the front door, only to realize Philip's limousine was around the back of the house. Then she'd have to find the driver and convince him to take her home, which seemed unlikely. The only logical solution was for her to find Eva and Martin. They'd have their driver take her home, even if it meant lots of questions, questions she would answer later.

She turned to go back into the throng when she felt a hand on her shoulder. To her surprise, she found Gene instead of Philip.

"Madalyn! What's wrong?"

How she produced a laugh, she would never know. "I'm getting a bit tired of that question," she muttered.

Desperation made a person do desperate things, she decided, but before she could talk herself out of it, she asked, "Gene, would you take me home?"

He hesitated for only the briefest second. "Certainly. My car is in the garage."

For the second time that evening, she saw the back of the house, only this time her emotions were churning with despair instead of anticipation.

Gene didn't say a word as he helped her into his low-slung sports car, except to ask for directions. She answered in a shaky voice and didn't argue when he helped her buckle her seat belt. She couldn't see to do it anyway, although she struggled to keep her tears from falling.

He reached into his back pocket and offered her a white handkerchief. She accepted gratefully, trying not to sniffle and show a complete lack of breeding.

He waited until they had entered her subdivision before he asked, "Are you going to be all right?"

She nodded. "Of course I'll be all right. I'm always all right."

"Can you tell me what happened?"

This time she shook her head. "Let's just say I've been given another painful lesson in humility."

He pulled into her driveway and shut off the engine.

"Because you're in love with Philip?" he asked, shifting toward her and resting his hand on the back of her seat.

Stunned, she pressed even farther back against the seat.

"Don't look so surprised. You positively glow when you're around him."

"I do?"

"Mmm-hmm. And tonight you lit up the whole room."

She picked at a pearl on her sleeve. "Please don't tell Philip," she whispered.

"If he's too blind to see, then far be it from me to help him." He paused. "Especially if he hurt you."

"Not physically, if that's what you're asking."

As he had been witness to the near conflagration in the study, she felt she owed him at least that much information.

The relaxation of the fist he had on his knee displayed his relief more eloquently than words. She knew the brothers weren't close, but she sensed Gene would have been devastated if Philip had somehow become the kind of monster that could hurt a woman.

"Gene, thank you for bringing me home. I'm sorry I took you away from the party."

"Are you kidding? I just wish I'd had a happier excuse to escape."

"Would you like to come inside?"

"No, thank you. I know you're being dutifully polite but I have the feeling you just want to get as far away from anything Ambercroft as you can." He nodded to her hand clutching the door handle.

She felt chagrin color her cheeks.

"Don't worry about it," he reassured her. "I understand."

"Thanks."

He looked thoughtful for a second. "What are you going to do on Monday?"

She hadn't thought that far ahead. She was barely functioning as it was.

"Clean out my desk, I guess. And start looking for another job."

"And what about your mother?"

She shot him a sharp look. "How do you know about my mother?"

"I talked to Philip while you were gone."

"Oh. Well, we'll make do."

For the first time, Gene seemed awkward.

"Come work for me," he blurted out.

"Pardon?"

"Just until you can find another job, a good job. I don't want you to have to rush and take anything you can find. Let me redeem the Ambercroft honor."

"Your offer is generous, but—"

"Don't decide right now. Go get some sleep and I'll call you tomorrow."

This time she did say goodbye and got out of the car. She couldn't stop Gene from walking her to the door, and she decided that maybe chivalry wasn't quite dead after all.

By the time the baby-sitter left and she locked up for the night, Madalyn was exhausted. But sleep wouldn't come.

Philip paced his room, waiting for Gene to get home...so he could punch his little brother in the nose.

After extricating himself from the men who'd delayed him from following Madalyn, he couldn't find her. He'd just happened to step out the front door to see Gene's Porsche heading down the driveway. The light wasn't good, but he'd assumed the female in the passenger seat had been Madalyn. A conversation with the footman at the door had confirmed his suspicions.

Tearing off his jacket, he threw it on the chaise longue. He nearly strangled himself getting his blasted tie off, although he probably deserved it.

He sat down on the edge of his bed, suddenly weary. He'd tried to call Madalyn several times, but kept getting her answering machine. He thought about driving over, but it was nearly midnight and she had a young child he needed to consider.

Besides, he deserved to wallow in his misery. There was no excuse for what he'd done. Even though he'd told her the truth about not using her for information, he should have told her about his interest in Price Manufacturing from the beginning.

Now she'd never trust him again. Hell, she'd never speak to him again. He'd wounded her pride.

Worse, he'd betrayed her trust.

The one thing she couldn't forgive... Not after what her other employer had done.

Gene never came home. Not an uncommon occurrence of course, but knowing he had last been with Madalyn only made Philip's imagination think absurd thoughts...thoughts no less disturbing even if they were crazy.

Sometime in the late hours of the morning, he finally fell into a fitful sleep.

Sunday was no better. When he still couldn't reach Madalyn by phone, he drove to her house, only to get no response to his impatient leaning on the doorbell. He heard no noise inside, and knowing how vocal

Erin was, he assumed Madalyn was out. Probably avoiding him....

He laughed at his own arrogance. She probably didn't think highly enough of him to believe he'd take responsibility for what had happened, much less try and reach her so soon.

Which left him nothing to do but quietly go crazy.

The thought of going back to the mansion was unappealing, so he headed to the office to try and bury himself in his work.

After a sleepless night and endless debates with herself, Madalyn decided in the early hours of the Sunday morning dawn to take Gene up on his offer.

She found out a lot about Gene in a very short phone call. Things she never suspected, such as he had a real job within the company. He oversaw engineering and feasibility studies on the many properties under consideration. He'd laughed when she'd paused, saying he was well aware of his reputation. He simply felt no need to defend himself, so few people knew he actually earned his salary. In that moment he had reminded her nearly unbearably of Philip. There was no lack of pride in that family, something she well understood.

She also learned that his office wasn't even in the same building as Philip's. His division was in another skyscraper a few blocks away.

After agreeing to talk the next day, they'd said their goodbyes and Madalyn had planned what she was going to do.

First of all, she had to get out of the house. She

was well aware of the incessant flickering of the answering machine, and she knew good and well the majority of the calls were from Philip. She wasn't a coward, but she had no interest in seeing the man today.

After a short drive and a long talk with her cousin, Madalyn decided to go to the office, type a letter to Philip and gather the few personal items she had left on the desk. With Erin happily playing, there was no time like the present, so with her cousin's blessing, Madalyn headed downtown.

Agreeing to work for Gene had not been an easy decision, but in the end, she'd gone back to the point that she wasn't a coward. More importantly, she hadn't done anything wrong. Adding in her concerns about her mother's pressing health care needs, Madalyn had started to get mad. She wasn't going to jeopardize her and Erin's future, and her mother's health, because Philip had turned out to be a heartbreaking disappointment. She knew her position with Gene was just another temporary assignment, but she would take it, and when she found a job at least comparable, she'd move on.

So that settled that. She was staying in Dallas, where she'd made a home for herself, where she was happy. She wasn't going to make any rash decisions, no matter how tempting it was to just pick up and go home.

She was a big girl now. No more dreams, no more fairy tales, no more head in the clouds. She thought she was over that, but obviously it had taken this giant whack upside the head from whatever powers that be to get it through once and for all.

The building was silent, as was to be expected on a Sunday afternoon. Her card key let her in and she gave a belated thought about her appearance—shorts, a tank top and sandals—but no one was going to see her, except the security guard who'd checked her card against her driver's license when she'd entered the building.

She had no sooner booted the computer when the door to Philip's office shot open, nearly scaring her witless.

"Philip!"

"Madalyn!"

"What are—" They spoke together.

Madalyn laughed ruefully. "Stupid me. I should have known you'd be here."

"Okay, we've now established that I have no life. So why are you here?"

"I was going to type you a letter filling you in on where to find everything I've done. Then I was going to get my picture of Erin and leave."

Philip shook his head. "Only you. You probably wish me someplace suitably hot and sulfurous, and yet you come in on a Sunday to do all that."

Madalyn closed her eyes and took a deep breath. She let it out slowly and looked up again. "I'm not angry with you. Anymore, that is."

"You're not?"

She shook her head. "I haven't had any sleep yet, which is why I look so bad, but the result of staying up all night is figuring out you didn't lie to me. You said you never pumped me for information, and that is true.''

He took a step closer. "Then why are you leaving?" He swept his hand toward the desk.

"Because this is more of a sin of omission than commission. You may not have used me, but you didn't tell me what you were up to, either. It's silly for me to feel I knew you, after such a short time working here, but I did. I trusted you, and the betrayal of that trust is more than I can take." She coughed a laugh. "You'd think I'd know better by now, wouldn't you?"

He looked at her for the longest time. "I'm sorry, Madalyn. I never meant this to turn out this way."

"I'm sorry, too, Philip." She smiled at him softly, sadly.

"I meant my promise. That you have a job at Ambercroft. This doesn't change anything."

"Thanks, but I have a job already."

"You do?"

"I'm going to work for Gene. For a while, anyway."

"Are you serious?"

"Perfectly."

He had clearly not been expecting that answer. It would have been funny if the moment hadn't been so sad.

He cleared his throat. "I wish you wouldn't go."

She busied herself at the desk. "It's not as though this is all that drastic for you, Philip. Mrs. Montague will be back Wednesday or Thursday, so you'll only have a few more days of upheaval."

He straightened, and as she watched, the old mask slipped over his face. "Of course. Do you need any help with your things?"

"No, there isn't much. Let me type up my report and I'll be out of the way."

"Certainly." He retreated to his office, stopping before he shut the door. "Do be sure and leave your key and access card with the guard on your way out."

Only the closed door heard her say, "Yes, sir."

The letter took longer than she anticipated, and the printout showed just how much she'd accomplished in a few short weeks. She left it on the printer and gathered her few things.

As she walked around the desk, it looked exactly as it had before. There was nothing to mark her passage.

But that wasn't why she was softly crying by the time the elevator doors closed and the car started its slow descent.

Philip heard the elevator bell chime and stayed seated. He'd been sitting there, unable to do anything but stare at the painted chopsticks he'd just found in his briefcase. They had slipped to the back, lying along the seam almost unnoticeable until he'd pushed his briefcase off the desk in a fit of pique and scattered the contents all over his floor.

At least picking up the mess he'd made had given him something to do.

A long time later, he opened his door and looked at the desk, now sanitized. He couldn't seem to move.

The longer he stared, the more bereft he felt because he finally accepted what he'd been denying.

He loved her.

And it was too late.

He trailed his hand along the wood, and then felt foolish. He felt doubly foolish when he realized he hadn't put down the stupid chopsticks, either. Deciding he needed a good, stiff drink, he keyed the elevator to go to the penthouse, and soon was nursing two fingers of thirty-year-old Scotch. Unfortunately, it didn't begin to dull the pain of knowing he'd lost the only woman he'd even really loved before he'd even had her.

Madalyn was everything he'd ever wanted in a woman. She was intelligent, witty and took him on his own terms. He wasn't a ticket to wealth and an entree into society. He was merely Philip. It was a hunger he'd had for so long, he'd grown numb to it, until Madalyn had made him dream again. Of possibilities.

She'd been eager to discuss the files he'd given her to work on. No one ever wanted to work *with* him, they were always too intimidated. Not Madalyn. She'd made his job exciting again, made his life exciting again.

That she was beautiful was merely icing on the proverbial cake. He knew she thought her figure was flawed, but she never talked about it the way he was used to, as a fishing expedition for a compliment. She might think her hips were too big, but he thought they were perfect. Just right for making love all night.

Not that he was going to get the chance to find out, but his body reacted to the mere suggestion.

Philip picked up the crystal decanter by the neck and headed for his west-facing balcony, slouching onto one of the lounge chairs to watch the sunset.

He left his glass in the living room.

Chapter Eleven

Madalyn struggled to get back into the routine. It wasn't that she hadn't worked hard with Philip—she had. This was different. She hadn't felt like she was going to a mere job then. Now, despite how kind Gene was, she didn't leap from bed each morning, anxious to get downtown.

Had it only been a week? It felt like a year had passed since she'd seen Philip. She was down to thinking of him less than a few thousand times a day, she guessed. The pain was worse, though. Maybe that meant it would start getting better soon.

The second week was no better. She stayed busy, but couldn't get over the underlying feeling of boredom. It wasn't Gene's fault. It wasn't anyone's. She felt more that a general miasma had settled over her, and she wondered if she'd ever feel alive again. It seemed Erin was the only thing that made her laugh anymore.

By the third week, even Gene couldn't stand it.

"Madalyn, I want you to do something for me. I want you to fly out to the new cabin we just bought in Aspen and outfit it for me."

"Pardon?"

"You heard me. We'll call it a working vacation."

"Gene, really—"

"I'm serious. I want you to decorate it and stock the place because I met this new lady I want to take there soon."

Madalyn smiled at him indulgently. Although not far apart in age, she felt rather maternal toward him. "Gene, you don't need me to do this. Surely you have someone—"

"I could hire a decorator, sure. But then, you're the one who needs some time alone."

She looked away, embarrassed that her moping was so obvious. She thought she had been doing a good job keeping a stiff upper lip and all that rot.

"You're sweet, but I'm a single mom. I don't ever get time alone."

"Well, I'm sure the mountain air will be good for Erin, too." His teasing smile turned serious. "Listen, Madalyn, I know you're not happy. Go to Aspen. Take a breather. When you come back, if you're not happy, I'll cut you a severance deal that will tide you over until you decide what you want to do next."

"Why?" she asked straight out. "You don't owe me this kind of treatment. It's more than generous, but I haven't earned it."

He nodded. "You're right. I don't owe you. I'm doing this because I like you and I want to. Enough arguing. I'll have the travel bureau book two tickets for you day after tomorrow. You and Erin go gather flowers in the Rockies and clear your head. You can have carte blanche on the cabin. We'll go over finance stuff later.''

The aching void in the region of her heart, growing bigger by the day, made her say yes. ''Okay, but we'll talk about that severance issue when I get back.''

''Great.'' He picked up the set of surveys he'd ostensibly come in for and turned to leave.

''Gene?''

''Yeah?''

''Thanks.''

Philip headed for his office and did a double take. After three weeks, it was odd that he was surprised to see Mrs. Montague at her desk. Some fantasy part of him kept expecting to glance over and see Madalyn.

Inexplicably he stopped. ''Mrs. Montague?''

''Yes, Mr. Ambercroft?''

Thirteen years. For the first time in thirteen years he was annoyed that she had never addressed him as Philip. She'd long ago said she felt it was improper, and he'd never argued with her.

''Sir?''

''What do you think our chances are on the Sanford merger?''

Her eyes grew round behind her glasses. ''I'm sure I wouldn't know, sir.''

Madalyn would have. She'd have given him her gut instinct, and the reason why. There was no reason to be irritated with Mrs. Montague because she wouldn't.

"Your coffee is on the credenza and the McConnally update is on your desk."

He nodded and entered his office, feeling out of sorts. This wasn't like him, but all he could think about was how Madalyn had never brought him coffee. Of course, he'd never asked for it, but that wasn't the point. Mrs. Montague might be the perfect secretary, but Madalyn had been the perfect...partner.

Two sharp raps on his door preceded Gene's entrance. Philip tried not to scowl, but doubted he succeeded.

"Here are the reports on the bank building in Austin you wanted."

"Okay. Now do you want to tell me why you delivered them yourself?"

Gene settled into one of the matching armchairs. "Just thought I'd tell you I sent Madalyn to Aspen."

"Aspen? Why?"

"Well, let's just say I told her it was because I needed her to decorate the cabin we just bought."

Philip didn't like the casual way Gene was studying his nails, nor the smile playing on his mouth.

"What does that mean?"

"Oh, nothing," he said with an abundance of innocence.

"Gene, if you're setting up one of your dalliances—"

"Dalliances? Jeez, Philip, is that word even used in this century?"

"Don't try to divert me, Gene. You'd better leave Madalyn alone."

"Why? You're not going to pursue her. She's a hell of a gal."

Philip didn't even know he'd gotten out of his chair. All he knew was he had dived for his brother, knocking the chair over backward, and now had Gene by the shirtfront. The anger coursing through him was overwhelming.

"I swear to you, if you so much as touch her, I'll—"

The fabric of Gene's shirt ripped beneath Philip's fingers.

All the teasing was gone from Gene's face. "You'll what? Hit me?"

Philip froze in place. His eyes cleared and he released Gene, surging to his feet. He stepped back and took deep, rasping breaths before the haze cleared. When his rage abated, he offered his brother a hand up.

He raked his fingers through his hair, the gesture awkward. "Gene, I—"

"Hey, that was just the reaction I was going for, bro."

Philip looked at Gene over his shoulder. "You what?"

"I've tried hinting, I've tried talking.... Nothing was getting through to you. So I decided to make you mad."

Philip snorted. "I'd say you succeeded."

"Go to her, Phi—"

"What on earth is going on in here?"

The imperious voice belonged to Olga Ambercroft. She cast a pointed gaze at the chair, at Gene's shirt, at Philip's hair.

"Good morning, Mother."

"Don't good morning me—"

"See, Mother," Gene cut in, giving his mother his usual, impertinent peck on the cheek. "I told you he loved her."

"Hmm. Philip, explain this."

"What's there to explain? I admit I'm in love with Madalyn, if that's what you're asking. But what difference does that make? She can't stand me."

"She's been miserable," Gene argued.

"You don't have to look so damn smug about it!"

"Don't you see, you big idiot? She's crazy about you. Go to Aspen. Talk to her. Make her marry you."

"Aspen?" Olga asked, looking between her two boys.

"I'll explain later," Gene assured her quickly.

Philip was still looking at Gene. "You may not have noticed this, but no one makes Madalyn do anything."

Gene just grinned.

"Philip," Olga said. "Go."

He looked at his mother.

"Don't think, just go."

She obviously misunderstood. He wasn't looking at her for encouragement, he was looking at her in amazement. "You're telling me you came all the way into the office to tell me to go ask a mere employee to marry me?"

She gave him an imperious look. "I came to here

to discuss the new trust agreement you sent me to sign. I can see, however, that Gene's suspicions are correct.''

"And it doesn't bother you that I'm in love with Madalyn?''

"It bothers me immensely,'' Olga said honestly, "but I'm smart enough to know that if you are this determined, my reservations are of little matter. My choices are to be stubborn and lose you, or wish you happiness and keep you in my life. I can only hope that Madalyn will not hold a grudge.''

"Very wise of you, Mother.''

"Be that as it may, I do wish you'd chosen a woman more suited, but I'm sure things will work out in time.''

"You can't choose who you fall in love with, you know,'' Gene offered, not unkindly.

"Yes, I know,'' Olga said, her face softening. "It may surprise you boys to know that I had no intention of ever dating your father, much less falling in love with him. But he could be very…persuasive.'' She gave herself a little shake. "Besides, this gives me hope of a grandchild before I'm too old to hold one.''

Philip felt his jaw go slack at this unheard-of glimpse into his mother's heart.

"Now,'' Olga continued, once more in complete control, "you'd best leave before I decide I'm being a sentimental idiot.''

"Yeah,'' Gene chimed in. "Go before I decide I'm the idiot and head for Aspen myself.''

Philip tossed his brother a grin and gave his mother

a kiss on the cheek. He didn't need any more prompting.

As he hurried out, he decided he had one phone call to make. Then he was going to win Madalyn's heart…and this was one joint venture he planned on lasting a lifetime.

After she got over her initial reticence about spending someone else's money, Madalyn had a marvelous time decorating the cabin. And to her surprise it was indeed a cabin. She'd been sure her definition of *cabin* and Gene's would be vastly different.

She had discovered two large rooms, one a bedroom, and the other a living/dining/kitchen combination.

The only item of furniture had been a brand-new bed in the bedroom, and she assumed the washer and dryer had come with the cabin. She ran the new sheets, which had been laying on the bed still in the packages, through a rinse cycle as she had no detergent, but it was good enough for the first night. She had had no idea if the cold nights were typical of spring there or not, but she was grateful for the beautiful quilt she'd also discovered on the bed.

The cabin was actually closer to a little town Madalyn had dubbed Paradise than it was to Aspen, and she was in love with it by the end of the second day. There probably was an actual town named Paradise in Colorado, if the rest of the state was as beautiful, but Madalyn didn't care. As far as she was concerned, she'd discovered the real one. Now that she'd actually set foot on this piece of the Rocky Mountains, she knew why people spoke so reverently of the experience.

She'd wasted no time. She already knew the owner of the coffee shop, a clerk at the little grocery and the gas station attendant by name. And everyone was in love with Erin.

She'd met with the owners of two small furniture stores and found out they were brothers and fierce rivals for the business usually brought by snowbirds revamping their vacation homes. She ordered a refrigerator and dining room set from Abe and an upright freezer and sofa set from Aaron. She decided she'd shop around some more for accessory pieces.

Window treatments were a tougher dilemma. She was engrossed in a specialty catalog when she heard a knock at the door and went to answer it. She had hoped the deliverymen would come after four so Erin could finish her nap, but—

"Philip!"

"Hello, Madalyn. May I come in?"

"Of...of course."

He stepped inside and glanced around. "It looks great."

She shrugged one shoulder modestly. "I tried to keep the masculine in mind, hence the earth tones in the furniture and rugs."

Philip faced her squarely. "Madalyn, I'm not here to talk about the decor."

Madalyn's stomach knotted as she realized why Philip was there. "Of course not. I can be packed in no time, but if it's all right, I'd like Erin to finish her nap."

"Dammit, I'm not here to evict you!" He took a calming breath. "Please sit down."

Philip took one end of the couch and she took the adjacent chair.

"I'm really nervous," he confessed, red staining his cheeks.

She could only stare. She felt like one solid bundle of nerves herself, but she was not expecting the same of Philip.

"Has something happened?"

"No. Yes. Oh, hell."

With obvious effort, he relaxed his hands and reached over to take her shaking ones.

"I've done nothing but think about you from the day I met you. I am so sorry about what happened, and I want the chance to make it up to you. I want another chance for us."

Madalyn was horrified. Maybe she should have seen it coming, but she hadn't. She jumped from the chair as though scalded and moved across the floor.

"No, Philip. Don't. Don't do this to me. There never was an 'us' and there never can be."

He followed her to the fireplace but didn't try to touch her.

"I thought we were working on an 'us' in the study."

"I was working on goodbye," she said quietly.

"I—"

"No, listen. This is crazy, and to be honest, I don't think I could survive another month like I've just been through. Please just go away and we'll pretend you were never here."

"I can't do that."

"Why not?" she asked desperately.

"Because," he answered, pulling her ghost-white knuckles from the mantel and kissing them, "I love you."

"You don't love me," she argued shakily. "You feel sorry for me, you want to take care of me and save me from my mundane existence, but you don't love me."

"Yes I do, and taking care of you is part of the package."

"But don't you see," she said, snatching her hand away and heading back for the chair, "I've been independent for a long time. I don't want anyone taking care of me. I don't need anyone to take care of me."

Philip captured her again and pulled her next to him on the couch. "What are you so afraid of?" he whispered urgently, holding her gaze with his own.

Tears, heavy and hot, began to roll down her cheeks. "I can't relinquish hold again, Philip, just because you charge in here on your white horse wanting to rescue me."

"What if I sign a prenuptial agreement promising never to spend any of your money?"

She laughed weakly and sank back against the cushion, resting her cheek on the crisp chintz. "You know this isn't about money," she admonished.

Slouching down, Philip mimicked her pose and moved his nose close to hers. "I know. So tell me what to do to convince you that I'm serious. Surely you're not going to try and argue class difference or some such nonsense."

"It is a consideration, you know."

"It is not. And we're not going to discuss it."

"Bully."

"Thank you. Now—"

"You aren't listening to me, Philip."

"And you're not listening to me." He put his fingertips against her lips. "You are perfect for the job of Mrs. Philip Ambercroft. I should know because I designed the specs for the job. And on top of that, I would dearly love to be a daddy to Erin. I know I have a lot to learn, but I'm determined to win the littlest Wier heart as well as yours."

Now he'd done it! The tears were back, and she dashed at them angrily.

"Don't use Erin—"

Philip caught her hand and finished wiping her tears away himself. "I'm not using Erin, honey. I'm trying to tackle all those arguments about why you can't marry me I see building up behind those beautiful eyes of yours. You've obviously forgotten how determined I can be about a merger, once I set my mind on it."

"Philip—"

"By the way, I've spoken with the Prices."

He succeeded in throwing her further off kilter.

"The Prices?"

"Mmm-hmm," he murmured, inching closer to trace his fingertip along her jawline. "Everything's going to be fine."

"They're going to let you help them? How did you manage that?"

"They were very open to it when they realized I'm almost family."

"Huh?"

"Sure. You're almost like a daughter, so I'll be almost like a son-in-law."

He took advantage of her stunned silence to lean closer the last bit and kiss her. He kissed her with all the hunger, passion, apology and need he had within him. He didn't stop until she was clinging to him. Then, reluctantly, he let her go.

She moved back a space so she could see his face again. "I'm not cut out for the shopping and tennis set."

"So keep working. Or open your own business. Isn't there something you've always wanted to do when you play 'what if'?"

That frightened expression was back, the one that said it was dangerous for her to play "what if," as if that were reaching beyond her grasp.

"Tell me," he urged.

"A nursery. I've always wanted to own a nursery."

"Okay, that's settled. Next?"

"Oh, Philip, you make this sound so easy."

"And why are you trying to make this difficult? I love you. I think you love me." He paused. "Don't you?"

"Love isn't always enough," she whispered hoarsely.

"It's enough to start on. I can't promise you we'll never have tough times. All marriages do. But I can promise you that I love you with all my heart and soul. I can promise you that I want to be a father to

Erin. I can promise you I want to give her brothers and sisters to play with. I can promise you—''

"Yes."

"Yes?"

"Yes, I'll marry you. I'm scared to death to risk it, but yes."

"Will you always make me crazy like this?" he asked, exasperated. "Putting me through hell, then all of a sudden just say yes?"

"Probably."

He clutched her to him and kissed her fiercely. "Well, thank God for that."

"How soon do you think we can get married?" she asked, and Philip's laugh filled the cabin.

Then he sobered. "Wait a minute. We can't."

"What?" she cried out.

"You haven't told me you love me."

"You big oaf. For that I shouldn't ever tell you."

He pressed forward and stretched out over her on the couch. "Say it."

She struggled not to smile. "I love you."

He closed his eyes in bliss. "Say it again."

"I love you."

The patter of little feet on the polished wooden floor had them both bolting upright. They peered over the back of the couch, swiveling as Erin came around the corner rubbing her eyes and clutching a well-loved rabbit.

When she saw Philip, she broke into a grin and ran for the couch, climbing into the space the adults had made for her. She promptly settled herself on Philip's lap, her back against his chest, and her thumb in her mouth. Giggling around her thumb, she stuck her foot out and rested it against her mother's stomach.

Madalyn melted. She didn't have any choice, not when facing this kind of barrage of love.

A thought struck her, and she rolled her head back against the couch, groaning.

"Madalyn, what is it?" Philip asked anxiously.

She cut him a grin and said, "Do you realize my mother was right? I got my Prince Charming after all. How am I ever going to live this down?"

Philip's laugh joined hers as they kissed over Erin's head.

"We'll find a way, honey. It'll be tough, but we'll find a way."

*   *   *   *   *

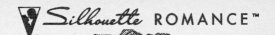

❤ *Silhouette* ROMANCE™

VIRGIN BRIDES

Your favorite authors tell more heartwarming stories of lovely brides who discover love... for the first time....

July 1999 GLASS SLIPPER BRIDE
Arlene James (SR #1379)
Bodyguard Jack Keller had to protect innocent Jillian Waltham—day and night. But when his assignment became a matter of temporary marriage, would Jack's hardened heart need protection...from Jillian, his glass slipper bride?

September 1999 MARRIED TO THE SHEIK
Carol Grace (SR #1391)
Assistant Emily Claybourne secretly loved her boss, and now Sheik Ben Ali had finally asked her to marry him! But Ben was only interested in a temporary union...until Emily started showing him the joys of marriage—and love....

November 1999 THE PRINCESS AND THE COWBOY
Martha Shields (SR #1403)
When runaway Princess Josephene Francoeur needed a short-term husband, cowboy Buck Buchanan was the perfect choice. But to wed him, Josephene had to tell a *few* white lies, which worked...until "Josie Freeheart" realized she wanted to love her rugged cowboy groom forever!

Available at your favorite retail outlet.

❤ *Silhouette*®

If you enjoyed what you just read,
then we've got an offer you can't resist!

Take 2 bestselling love stories FREE!

Plus get a FREE surprise gift!

Clip this page and mail it to Silhouette Reader Service™

IN U.S.A.
3010 Walden Ave.
P.O. Box 1867
Buffalo, N.Y. 14240-1867

IN CANADA
P.O. Box 609
Fort Erie, Ontario
L2A 5X3

YES! Please send me 2 free Silhouette Romance® novels and my free surprise gift. Then send me 6 brand-new novels every month, which I will receive months before they're available in stores. In the U.S.A., bill me at the bargain price of $2.90 plus 25¢ delivery per book and applicable sales tax, if any*. In Canada, bill me at the bargain price of $3.25 plus 25¢ delivery per book and applicable taxes**. That's the complete price and a savings of over 10% off the cover prices—what a great deal! I understand that accepting the 2 free books and gift places me under no obligation ever to buy any books. I can always return a shipment and cancel at any time. Even if I never buy another book from Silhouette, the 2 free books and gift are mine to keep forever. So why not take us up on our invitation. You'll be glad you did!

215 SEN CNE7
315 SEN CNE9

Name	(PLEASE PRINT)	
Address	Apt.#	
City	State/Prov.	Zip/Postal Code

* Terms and prices subject to change without notice. Sales tax applicable in N.Y.
** Canadian residents will be charged applicable provincial taxes and GST.
  All orders subject to approval. Offer limited to one per household.
  ® are registered trademarks of Harlequin Enterprises Limited.

SROM99   ©1998 Harlequin Enterprises Limited

Don't miss Silhouette's newest cross-line promotion,

Four royal sisters find their own Prince Charmings as they embark on separate journeys to find their missing brother, the Crown Prince!

The search begins in October 1999 and continues through February 2000:

On sale October 1999: **A ROYAL BABY ON THE WAY** by award-winning author **Susan Mallery** (Special Edition)

On sale November 1999: **UNDERCOVER PRINCESS** by bestselling author **Suzanne Brockmann** (Intimate Moments)

On sale December 1999: **THE PRINCESS'S WHITE KNIGHT** by popular author **Carla Cassidy** (Romance)

On sale January 2000: **THE PREGNANT PRINCESS** by rising star **Anne Marie Winston** (Desire)

On sale February 2000: **MAN...MERCENARY...MONARCH** by top-notch talent **Joan Elliott Pickart** (Special Edition)

ROYALLY WED
Only in—
SILHOUETTE BOOKS

Available at your favorite retail outlet.

Visit us at www.romance.net

SSERW